# THE 117-STOREY TREEHOUSE

Andy Griffiths lives in a 117-storey treehouse with his friend Terry and together they make funny books, just like the one you're holding in your hands right now. Andy writes the words and Terry draws the pictures. If you'd like to know more, read this book (or visit www.andygriffiths.com.au).

Terry Denton lives in a 117-storey treehouse with his friend Andy and together they make funny books, just like the one you're holding in your hands right now. Terry draws the pictures and Andy writes the words. If you'd like to know more, read this book (or visit www.terrydenton.com).

*Climb higher every time*
*with the Treehouse series*

# ANDY GRIFFITHS

# THE 117-STOREY TREEHOUSE

ILLUSTRATED BY

# TERRY DENTON

MACMILLAN CHILDREN'S BOOKS

Hee, haw!

First published 2019 by Pan Macmillan Australia Pty Limited

First published in the UK 2019 by Macmillan Children's Books
an imprint of Pan Macmillan
20 New Wharf Road, London N1 9RR
Associated companies throughout the world
www.panmacmillan.com

ISBN 978-1-5098-8527-5

Text copyright © Flying Beetroot Pty Ltd 2019
Illustrations copyright © Terry Denton 2019

The right of Andy Griffiths and Terry Denton to be identified as
th_____ _____ _____ _____ _____ _____ in
_____ with the Copyright, Designs and Patents Act _____.

The author _____ _____ _____ _____ _____ _____cted with or
sponsored by _____ _____ _____ _____ _____ _____ - and including
_____ relation to which they _____ _____ _____ _____.

A_____ ed,
stor _____ _____ _____ _____ _____ _____ _____ _____neans
_____ _____ _____ _____ _____ _____ _____),
_____ _____ _____ _____ _____ _____ _____

Pan _____ _____ _____ _____ _____ty for,
_____ _____ _____ _____ _____ _____k.

A CIP catalogue record for this book is available from the British Library.

Typeset in 14/18 Minion Pro by Seymour Designs
Printed and bound by CPI Group (UK) Ltd, Croydon CR0 4YY

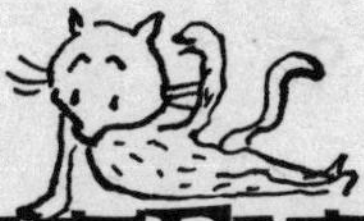

# CONTENTS



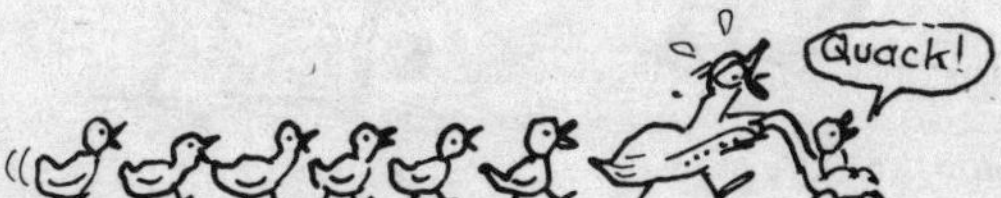

Quack!

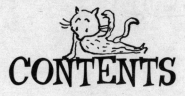

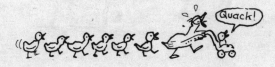

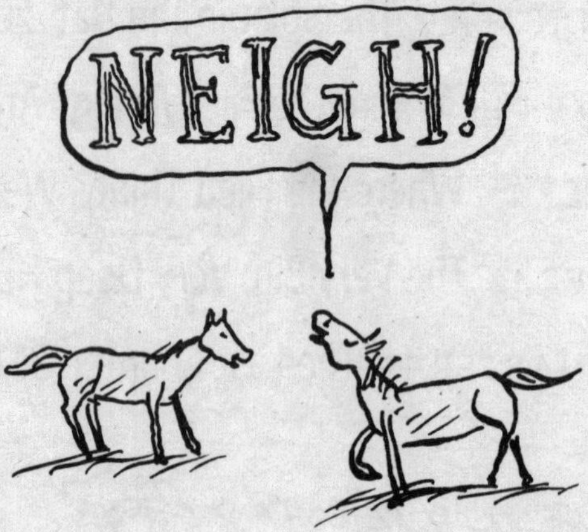
NEIGH!

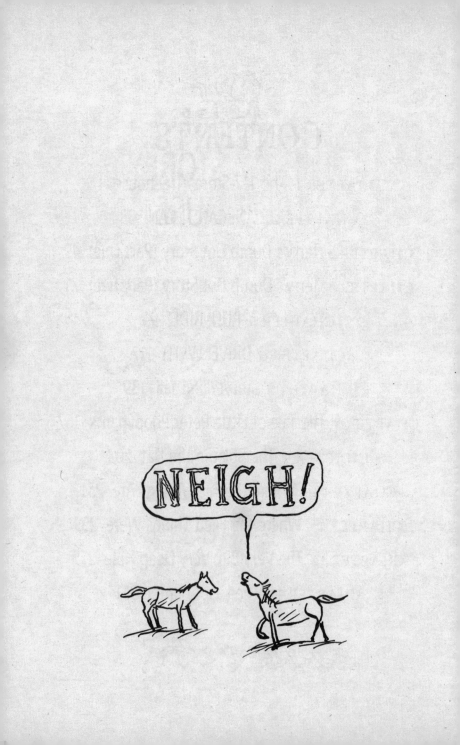

## CHAPTER 1

# THE 117-STOREY TREEHOUSE

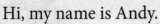

Hi, my name is Andy.

This is my friend Terry.

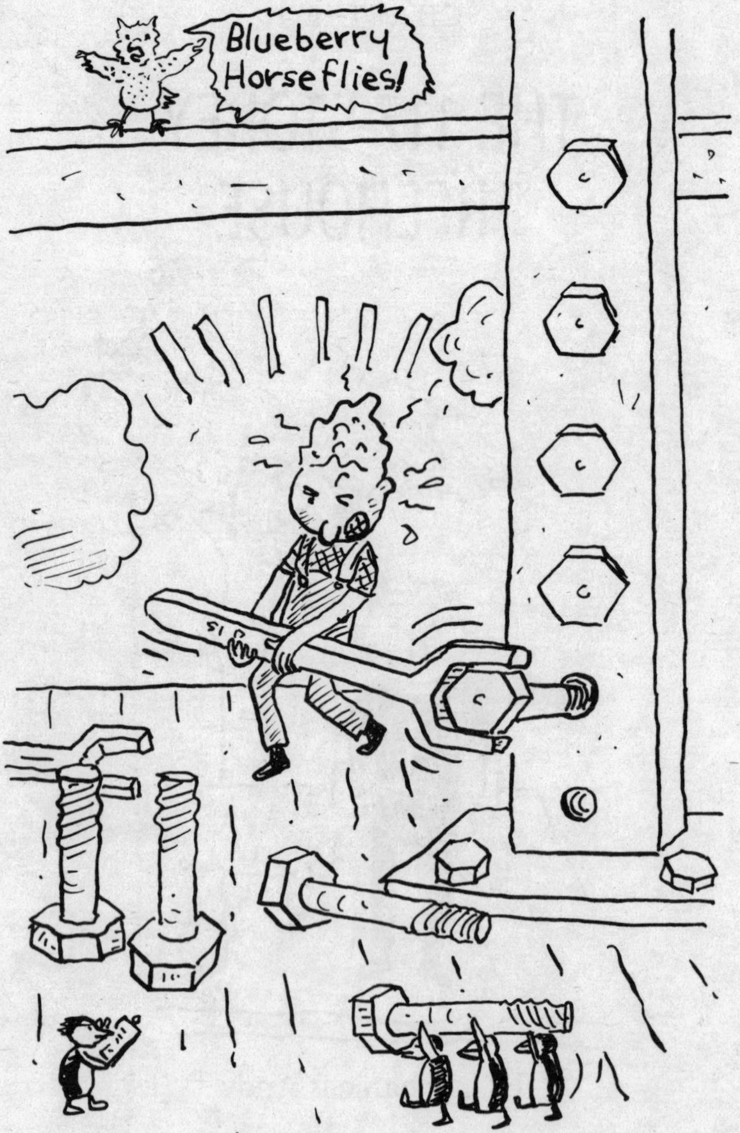
Blueberry Horseflies!

We live in a tree.

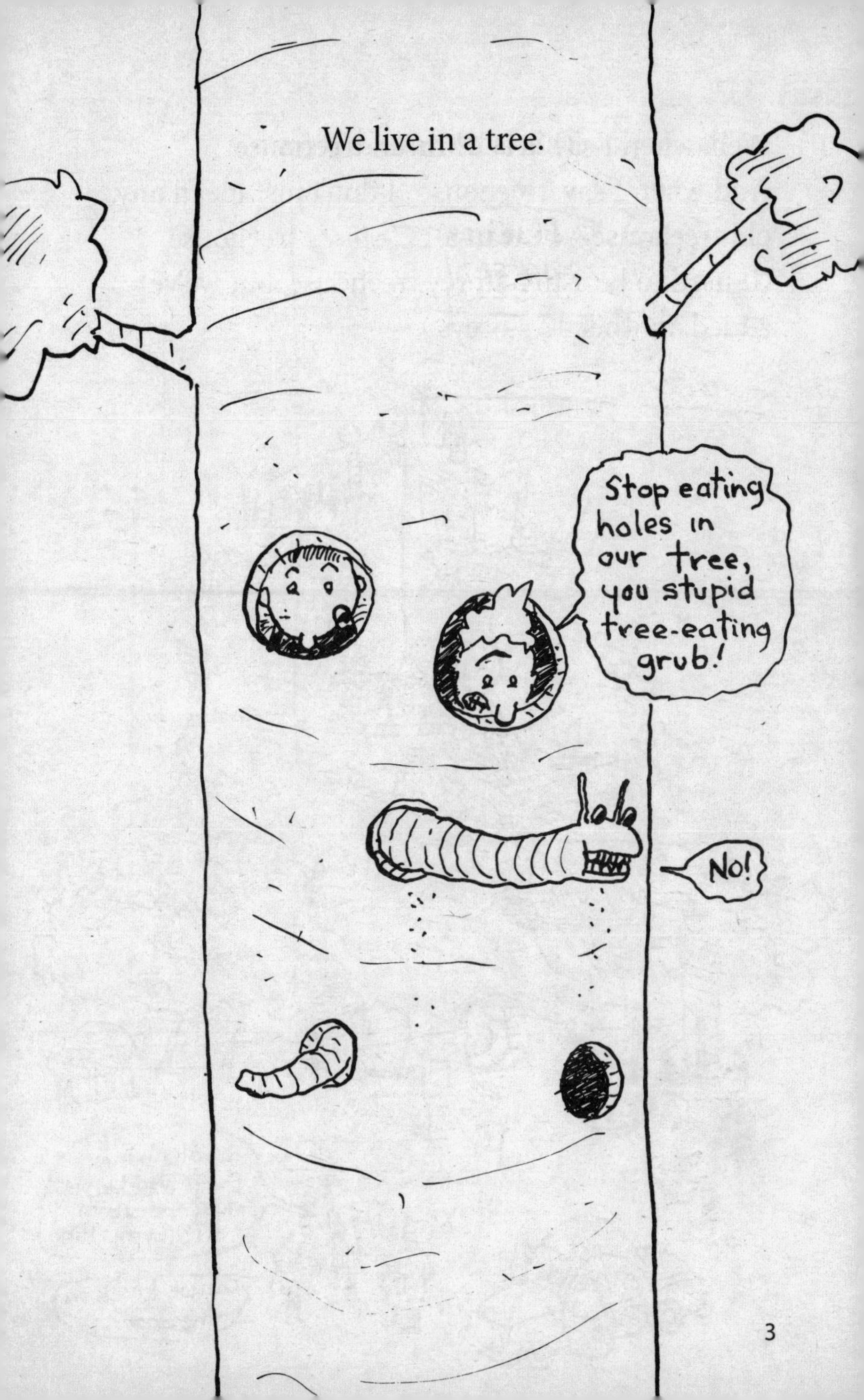
Stop eating holes in our tree, you stupid tree-eating grub!
No!

Well, when I say 'tree', I mean treehouse.
And when I say 'treehouse', I don't just mean any
old treehouse—I mean a 117-*storey* treehouse.
(It used to be a 104-storey treehouse, but we've
added another 13 storeys.)

So what are you waiting for?
Come on up!

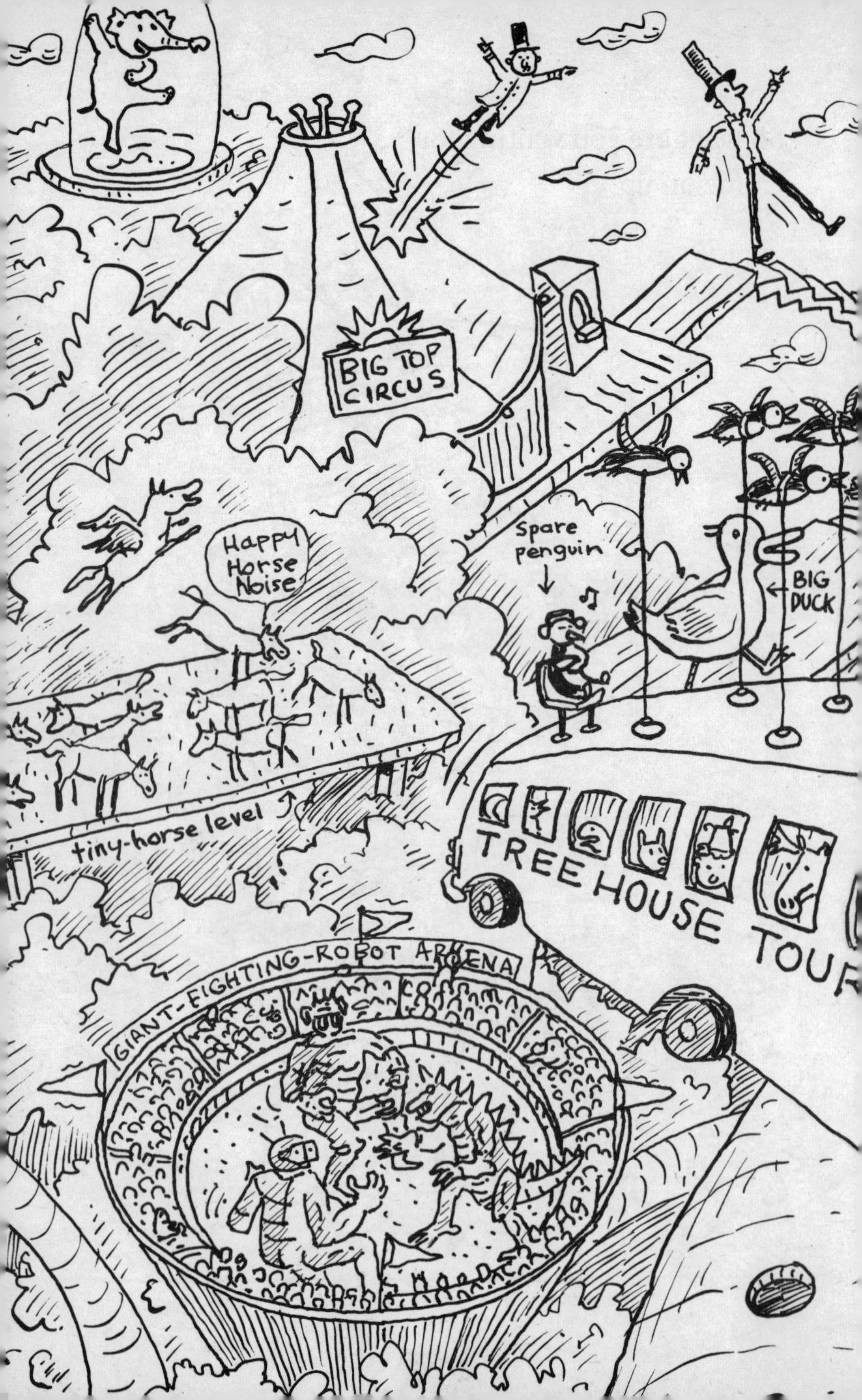
BIG TOP CIRCUS
Happy Horse Noise
Spare penguin
BIG DUCK
tiny-horse level
TREE HOUSE TOUR
GIANT-FIGHTING-ROBOT ARENA

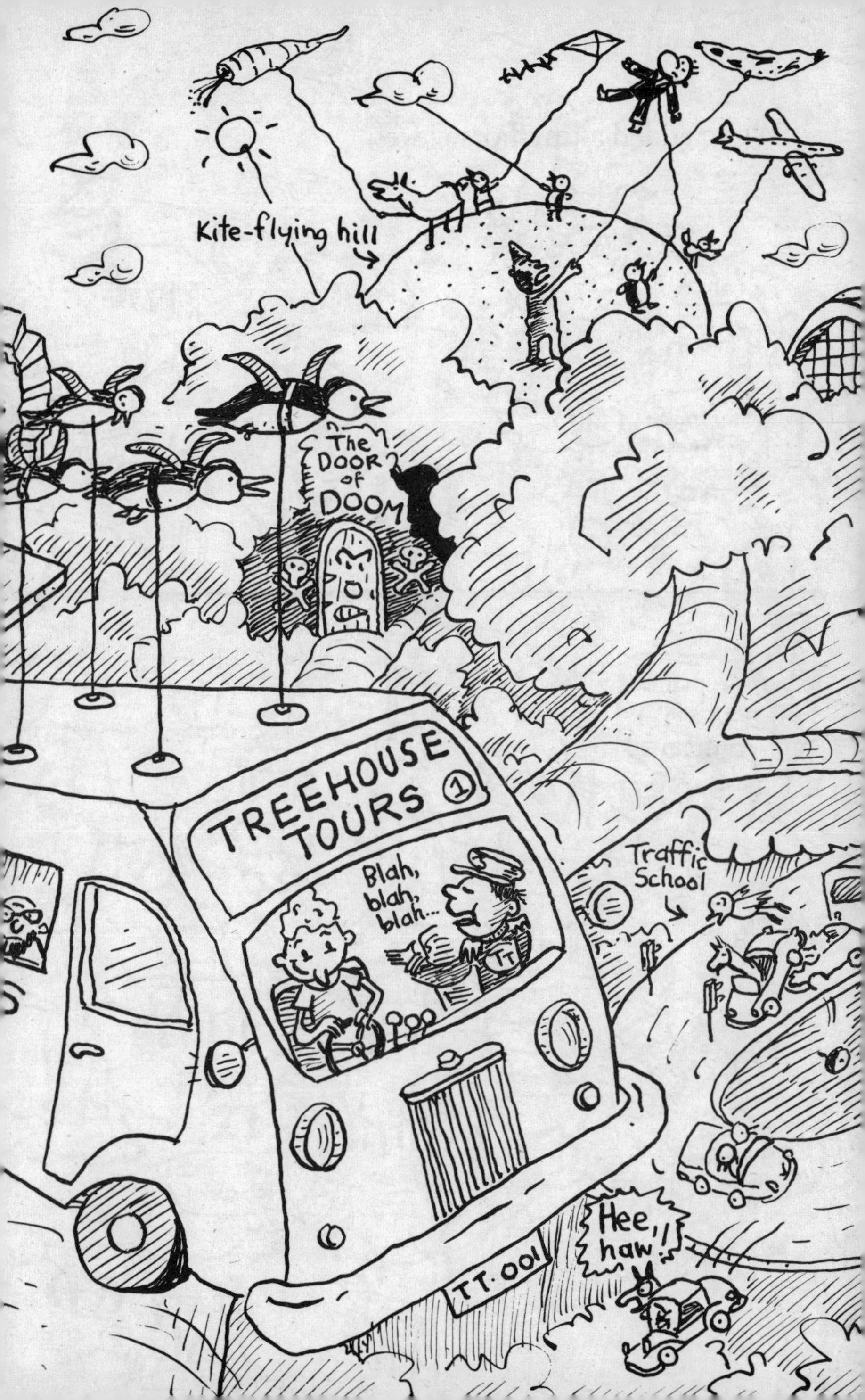
Kite-flying hill
The DOOR of DOOM
TREEHOUSE TOURS 1
Blah, blah, blah...
TT
Traffic School
Hee, haw!
TT·001

We've added a tiny-horse level,

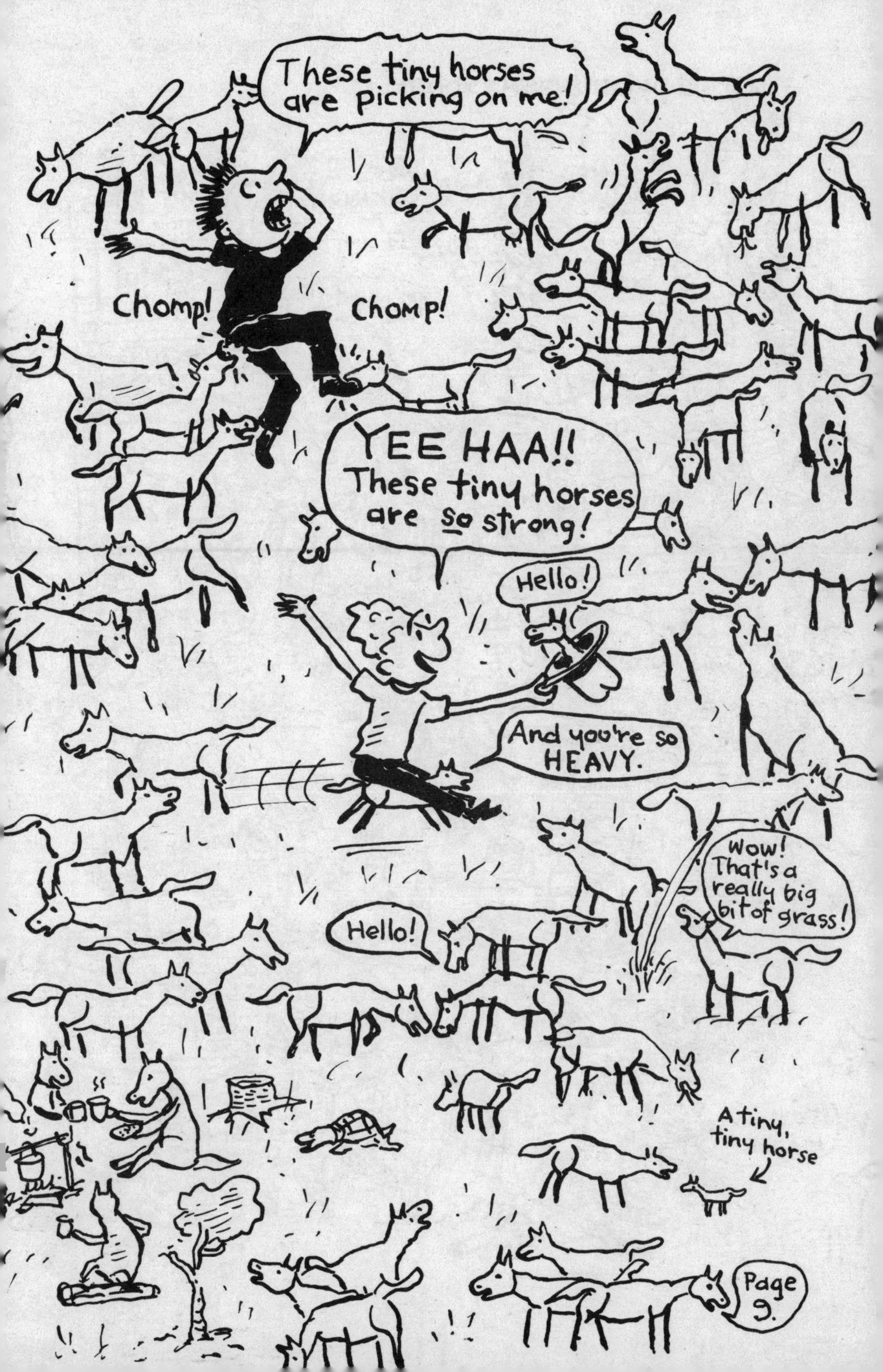
These tiny horses are picking on me!
Chomp!
Chomp!
YEE HAA!! These tiny horses are so strong!
Hello!
And you're so HEAVY.
Wow! That's a really big bit of grass!
Hello!
A tiny, tiny horse
Page 9.

a pyjama-party room,

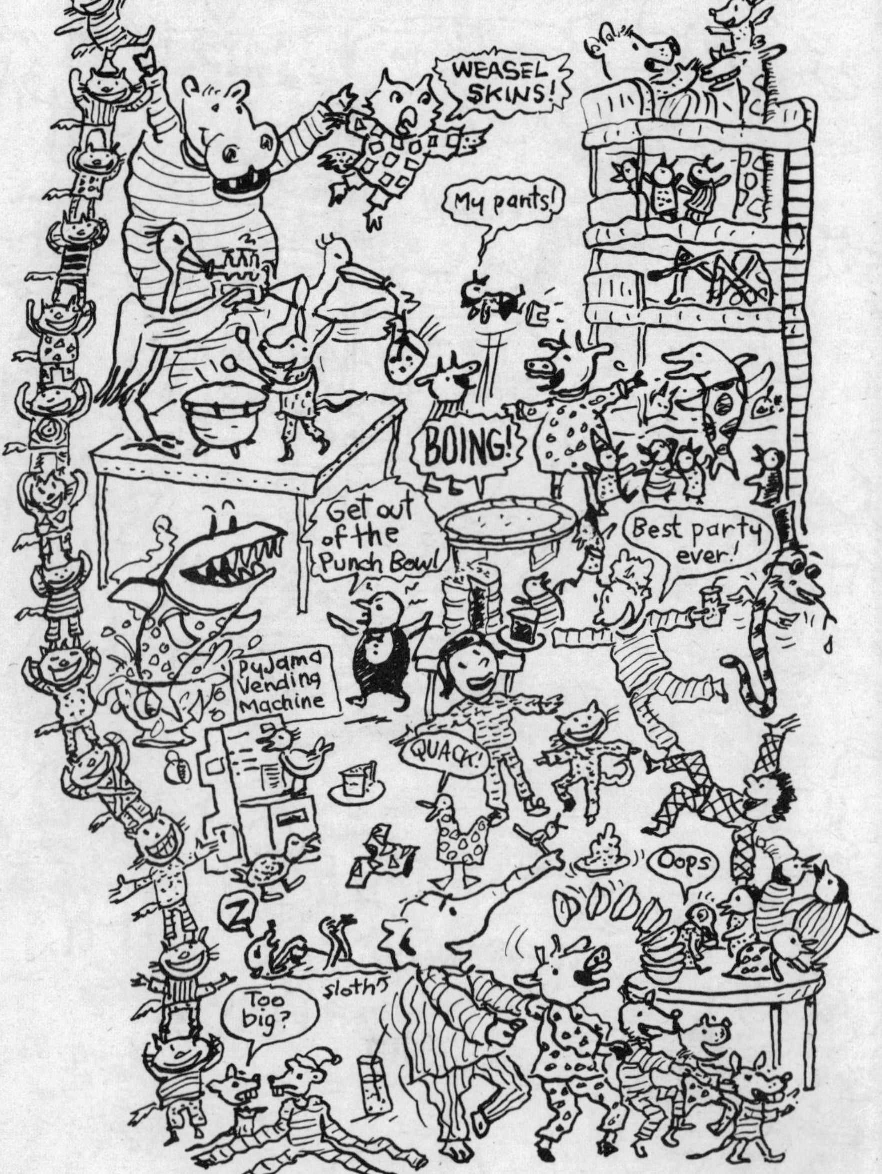
WEASEL SKINS!
My pants!
BOING!
Get out of the Punch Bowl
Best party ever!
Pyjama Vending Machine
QUACK!
Oops
Z
sloths
Too big?

an Underpants Museum,

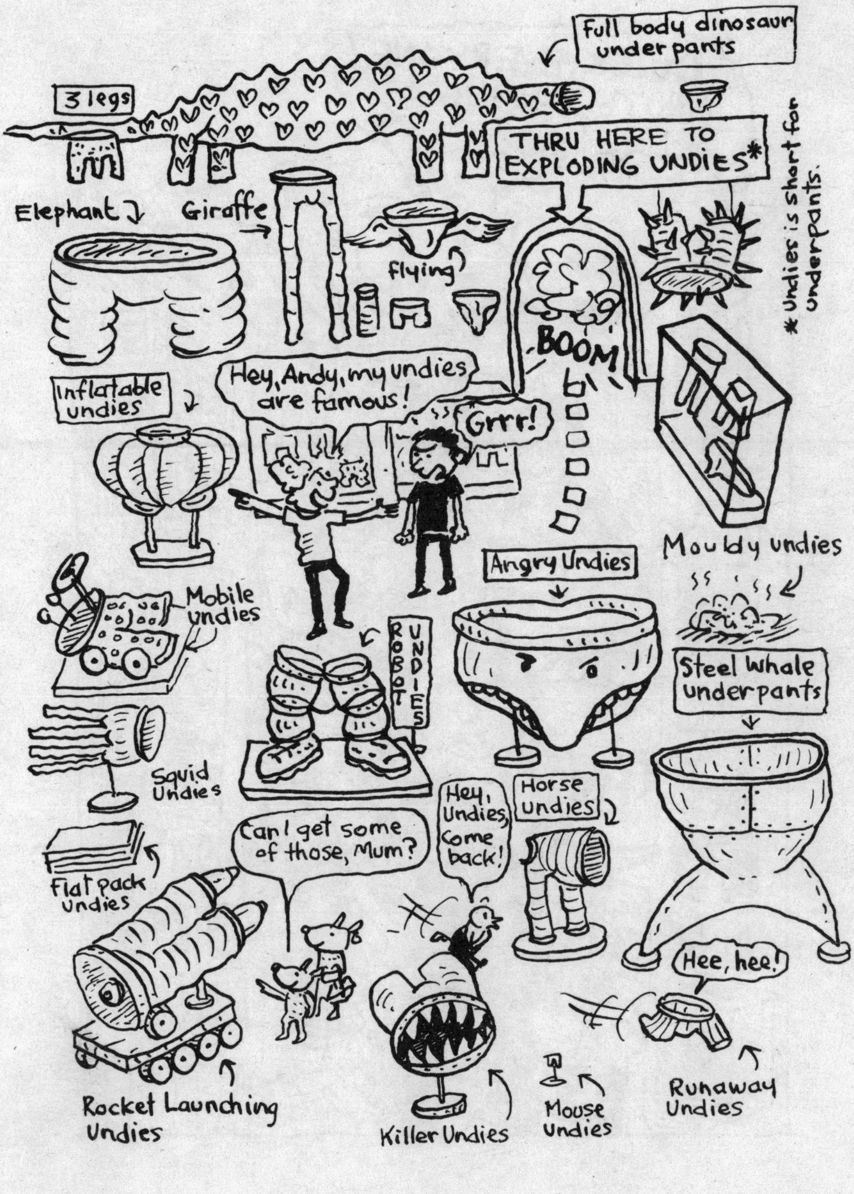

Full body dinosaur underpants
3 legs
THRU HERE TO EXPLODING UNDIES*
* Undies is short for underpants.
Elephant
Giraffe
flying
BOOM
Hey, Andy, my undies are famous!
Grrr!
Inflatable undies
Mouldy undies
Angry Undies
Mobile undies
ROBOT UNDIES
Steel whale underpants
Squid Undies
Hey, Undies, come back!
Horse undies
Can I get some of those, Mum?
Flat pack undies
Hee, hee!
Rocket Launching Undies
Killer Undies
Mouse Undies
Runaway Undies

a photo-bombing booth,

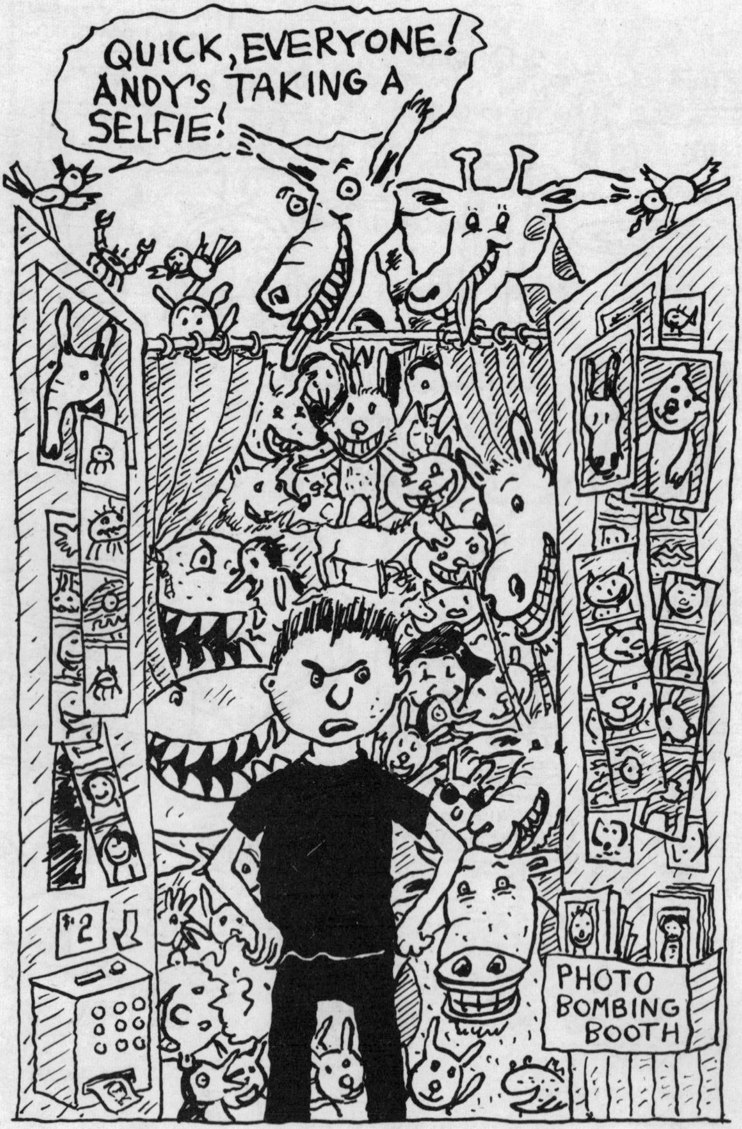
QUICK, EVERYONE! ANDY'S TAKING A SELFIE!
$2
PHOTO BOMBING BOOTH

a waiting room,

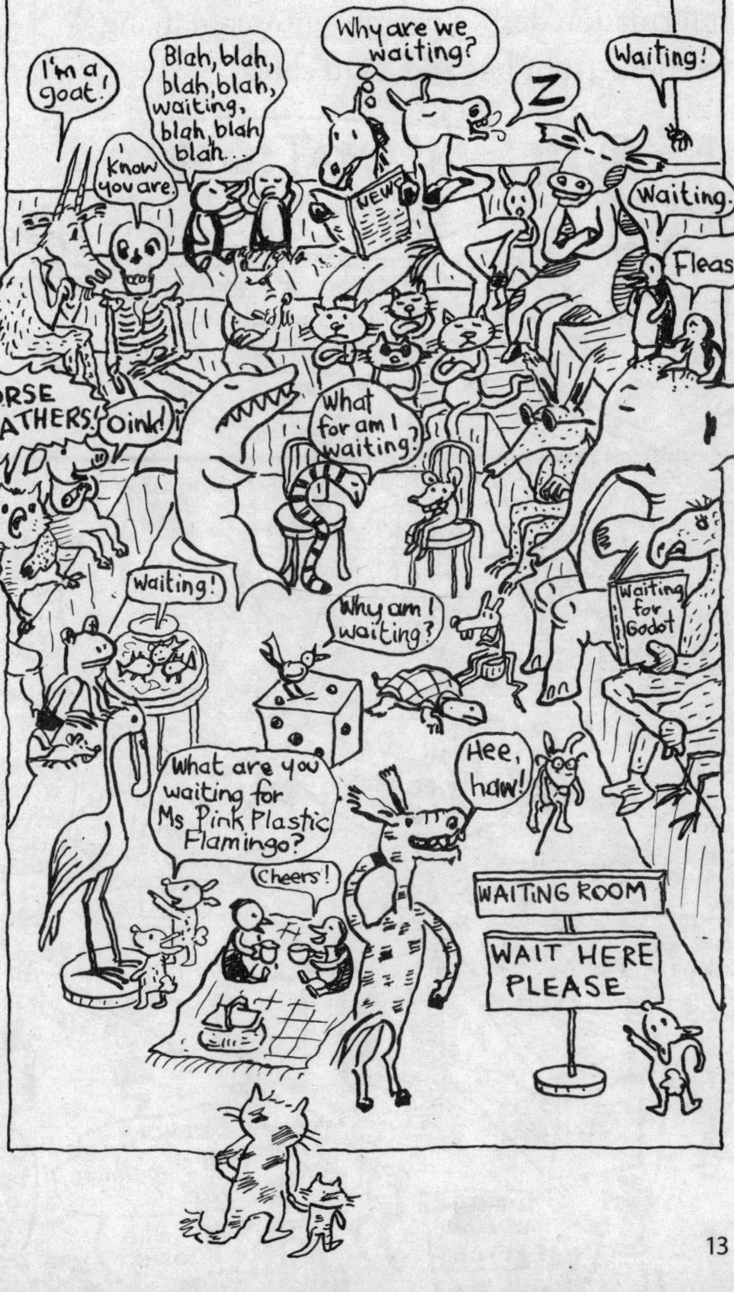
I'm a goat!
Know you are.
Blah, blah, blah, blah, waiting, blah, blah blah...
NEWS
Why are we waiting?
Z
Waiting!
Waiting.
Fleas!
HORSE FEATHERS!
Oink!
What for am I waiting?
Waiting for Godot
Waiting!
Why am I waiting?
What are you waiting for Ms Pink Plastic Flamingo?
Hee, haw!
Cheers!
WAITING ROOM
WAIT HERE PLEASE

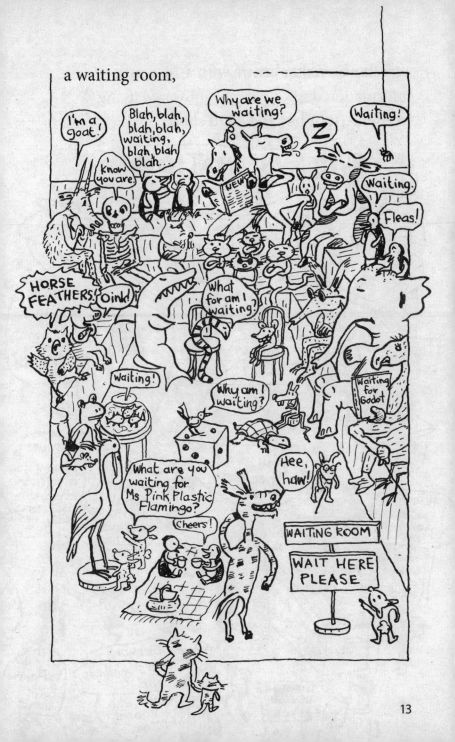

a treehouse visitor centre with a 24-hour information desk, a penguin-powered flying treehouse tour bus and a gift shop,

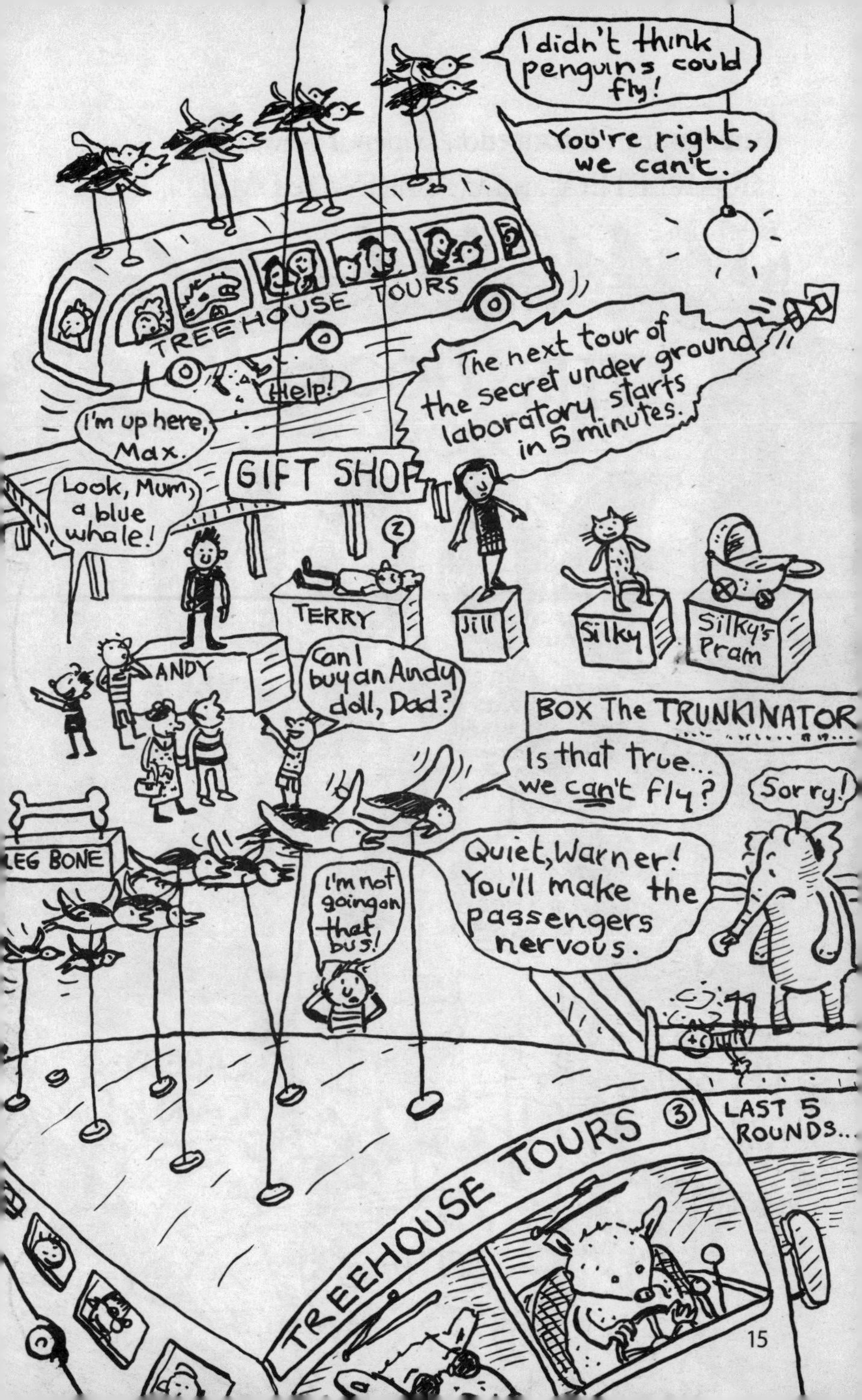
I didn't think penguins could fly!
You're right, we can't.
TREEHOUSE TOURS
Help!
I'm up here, Max.
The next tour of the secret under ground laboratory starts in 5 minutes.
GIFT SHOP
Look, Mum, a blue whale!
TERRY
Jill
Silky
Silky's Pram
ANDY
Can I buy an Andy doll, Dad?
BOX The TRUNKINATOR
Is that true... we can't fly?
Sorry!
LEG BONE
Quiet, Warner! You'll make the passengers nervous.
I'm not going on that bus!
TREEHOUSE TOURS 3
LAST 5 ROUNDS...
TREEHOUSE TOURS

the Door of Doom (don't open it or you'll be COMPLETELY and UTTERLY DOOMED!),

a circus with fire-eaters, sword-swallowers, chair-tamers, trapeze artists and clowns,

an all-you-can-eat-including-the-furniture level where you can eat absolutely everything, including the furniture,

a kite-flying hill,

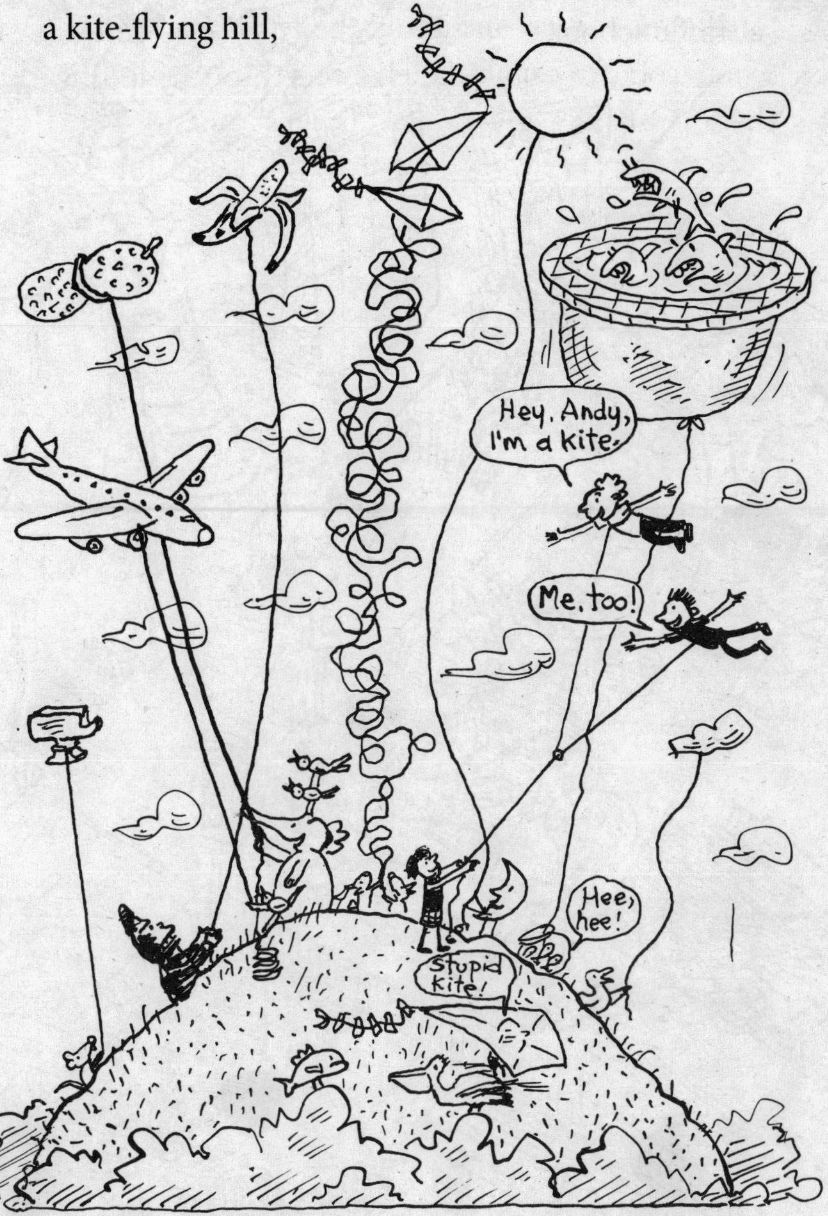
Hey, Andy, I'm a kite.
Me, too!
Hee, hee!
Stupid kite!

a traffic school,

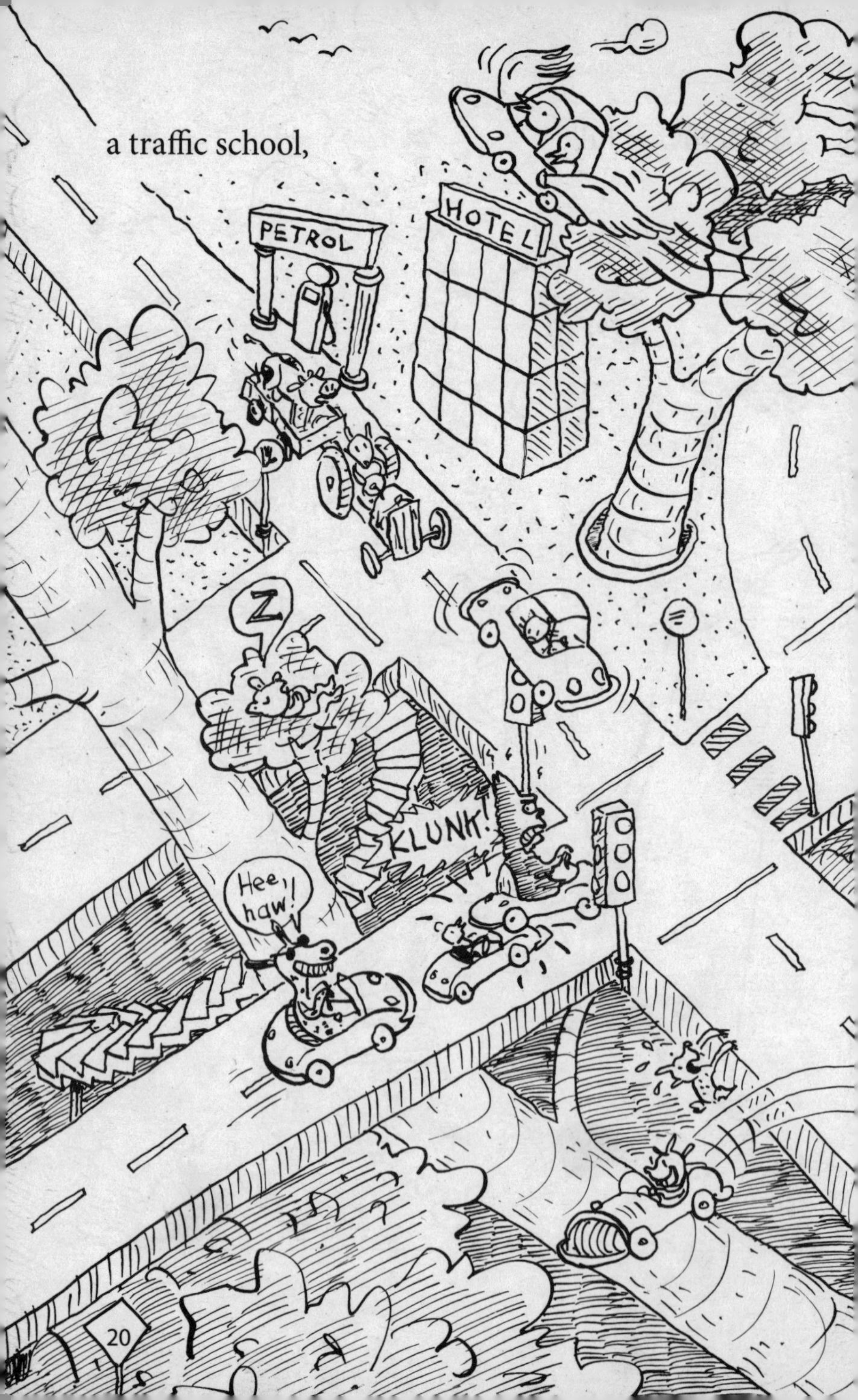
PETROL
HOTEL
Z
KLUNK!
Hee, haw!

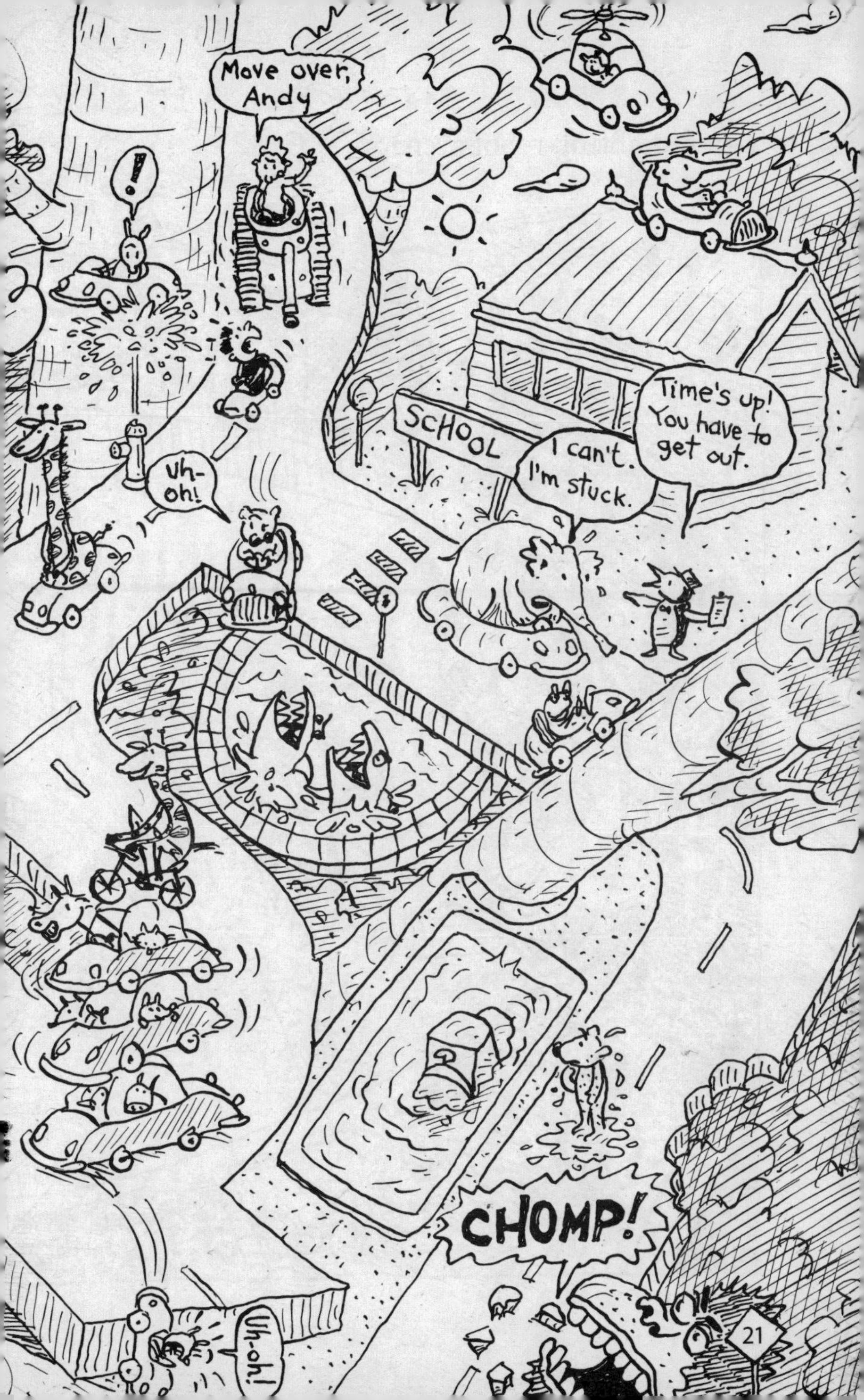

Move over, Andy
!
Uh-oh!
SCHOOL
Time's up! You have to get out.
I can't. I'm stuck.
CHOMP!
Uh-oh!

a giant-fighting-robot arena,

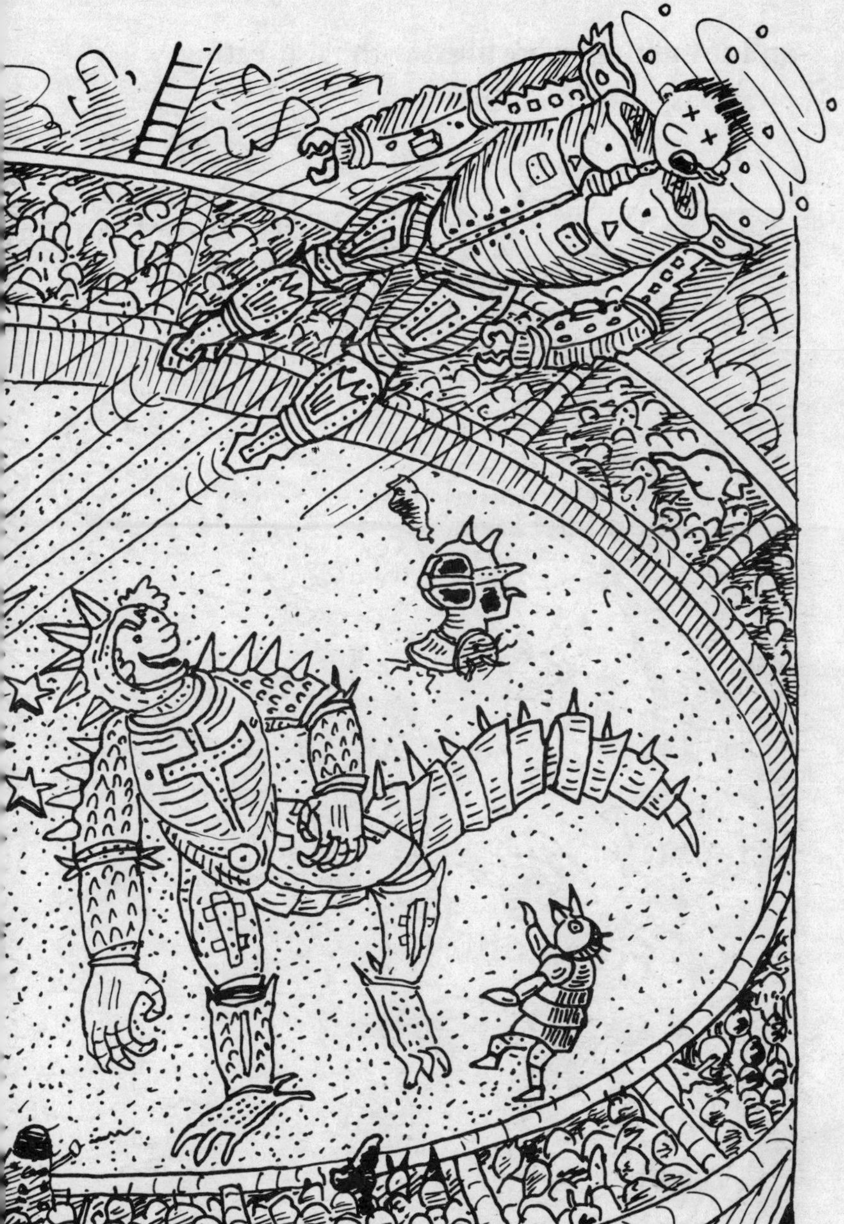

and a water-ski park filled with flesh-eating piranhas—don't fall in!

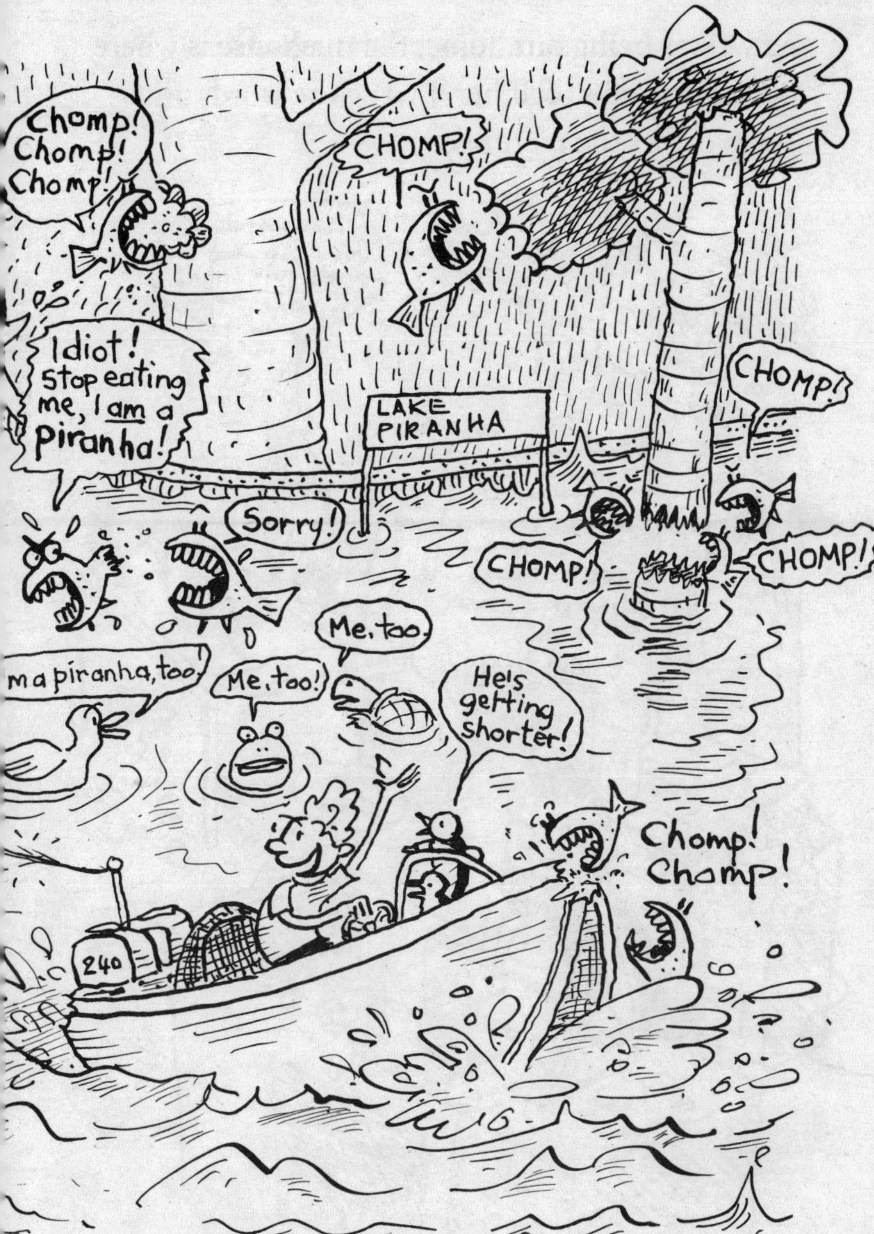
Chomp! Chomp! Chomp!
CHOMP!
Idiot! Stop eating me, I am a piranha!
LAKE PIRANHA
CHOMP!
Sorry!
CHOMP!
CHOMP!
Me, too.
ma piranha, too.
Me, too!
He's getting shorter!
Chomp! Chomp!

As well as being our home, the treehouse is where we make books together. I write the words and Terry draws the pictures.

As you can see, we've been doing this for quite a while now.

It can get a little crazy at times …

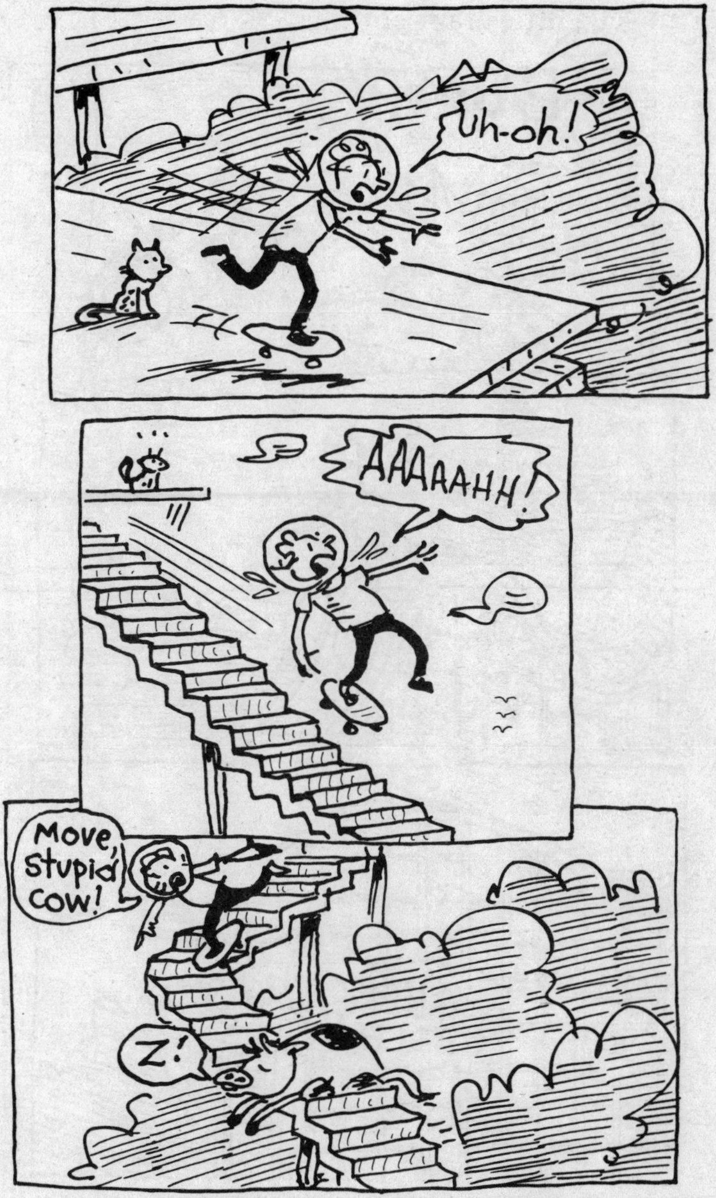
Uh-oh!
AAAAAHH!
Move, stupid cow!
Z!

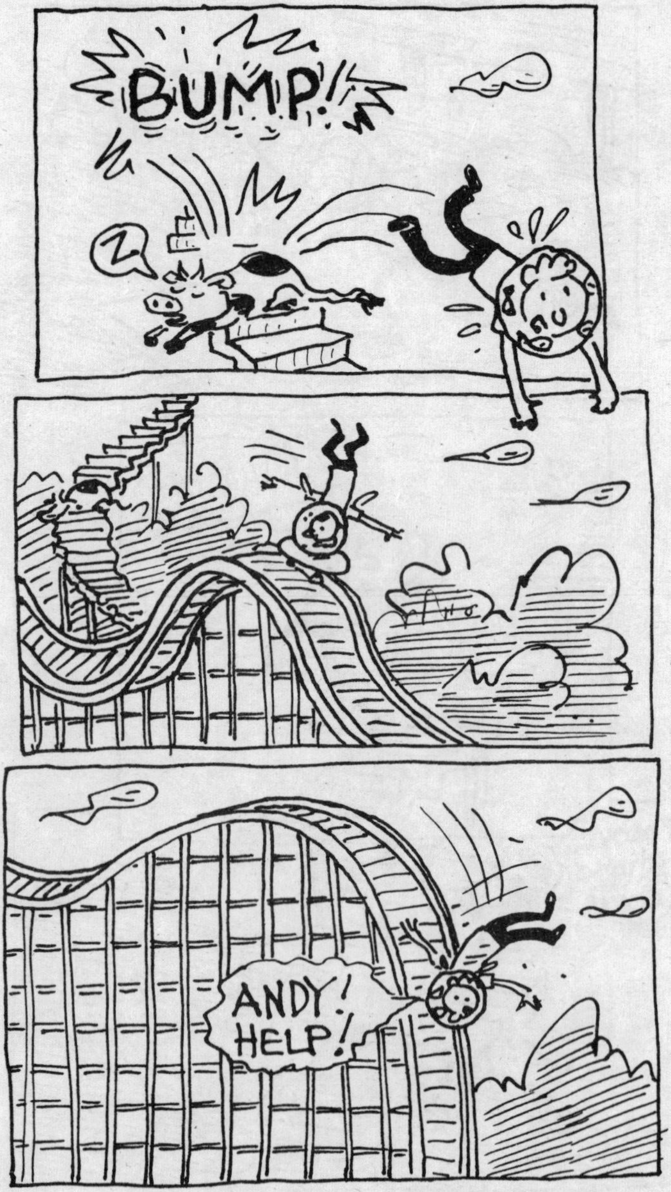
BUMP!
ANDY! HELP!

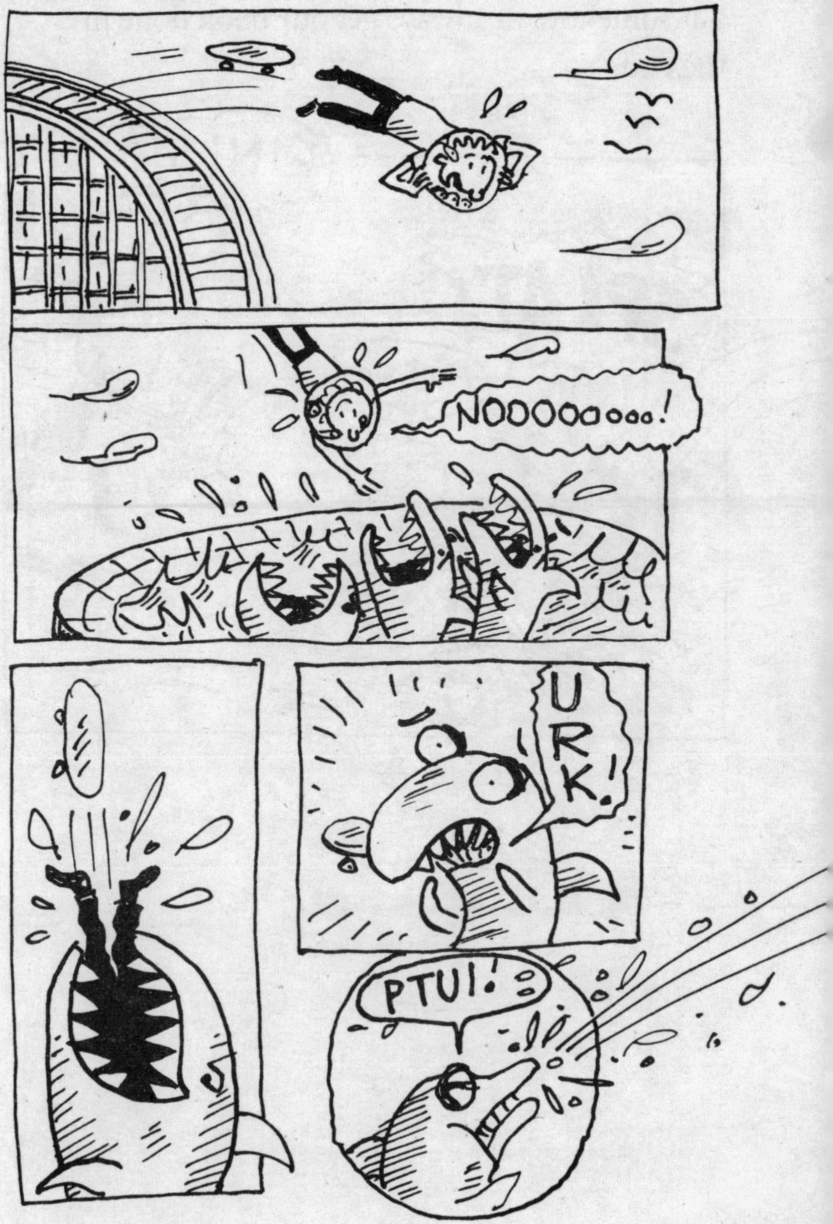
NOOOOOooo!
URK!
PTUI!

but somehow we always get our book done in the end.

## CHAPTER 2

# CAN! CAN'T! CAN!

If you're like most of our readers, you're probably wondering how come it's always me who tells the story and never Terry.

'Yeah,' says Terry. 'I've wondered that too. How come I never get to tell the story?'

'Because I'm the narrator,' I say, 'and you're the illustrator—that's why!'

'I can narrate too, you know,' says Terry.

'No you can't,' I say.

'Yes I can!' says Terry.

'CAN'T!'

'CAN!'

'CAN'T!'

'CAN!'

'CAN'T!'

'CAN!'

'CAN'T!'

'CAN!'

# 'CAN'T!'

'CAN!'

I'm just about to yell 'CAN'T' even bigger when Jill comes along.

'What are you two arguing about?' she says.

'Terry says he can narrate and I say he

# CAN'T!'

'There's a better way to settle this than by shouting at each other,' says Jill.

'*Really?*' I say. 'How?'

'Let Terry do some narration and see how it goes,' says Jill.

'But he's an illustrator. Illustrators can't narrate—*everybody* knows that!'

'That's not true,' says Jill. 'What about Dr Moose? He wrote *and* illustrated *The Splat in the Hat*.'

'And who could forget the wonderful Beatrix Potty?' says Jill. 'I *love* her animal stories—and she does the story and the illustrations as well!'

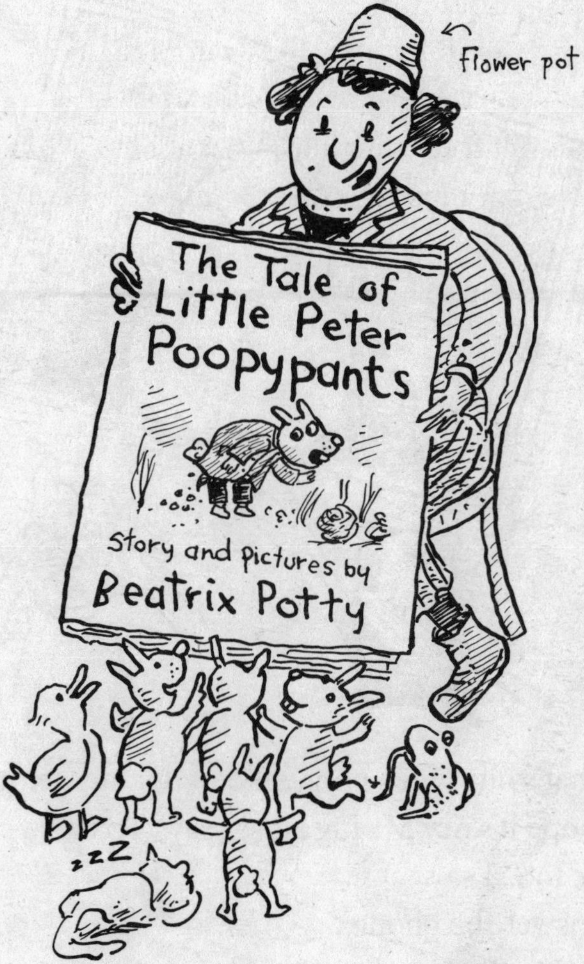
Flower pot
The Tale of Little Peter Poopypants
Story and pictures by
Beatrix Potty
zzZ

**RING! RING!**
**RING! RING!**
**RING! RING!**

Oh, that's our video phone. I'd better answer it.

'I hope it's not Mr Big Nose,' says Terry.

'Me too,' I say.

I answer the phone.

It *is* Mr Big Nose!

'Why hasn't the story started yet?' he says.

'Because,' I say, 'Terry wants to tell the story and I was just explaining that illustrators can't tell stories because that's the author's job.'

'That's nonsense!' says Mr Big Nose. 'What about Boris Bendback? His *Where the Filed Things Are* is the most famous and best-loved children's book about office management of *all* time ... and he's the author *and* the illustrator!'

'Yeah,' I say, 'that is good, but—'

'No buts about it,' says Mr Big Nose. 'If Terry wants to tell the story then let him—maybe he'll create a classic just like Boris Bendback. But make sure it's on my desk by five o'clock this afternoon … or I'll file you both under F for FIRED!'

'Don't worry about a thing,' I say. 'We'll get it done.'

'You'd better!' says Mr Big Nose.

The screen goes blank.

'Yay!' says Terry. 'Mr Big Nose said I can tell the story!'

I shake my head. 'Are you sure you want to do this, Terry? Storytelling is not as simple as it looks, you know. You can get into quite a lot of trouble, actually. If you do anything wrong, the Story Police could arrest you and put you in prison.'

'What for?' says Terry.

'For crimes against storytelling,' I say.

'I don't believe you,' says Terry. 'There's no such thing as Story Police.'

'There is so!' I say. 'And if you do anything they don't like they'll come after you and then you'll be sorry.'

'You're just saying that because you don't want me to tell the story,' says Terry.

'No, I'm not,' I say. 'They really *do* exist. You believe me, don't you, Jill?'

'Not really,' says Jill.

'Fine,' I say. 'Tell the story, Terry. But don't say I didn't warn you.'

'Okay, here goes ...' says Terry.

In the beginning
there was a ...
um ... um ...
well ...

now ... er ... ah
... well ... it's like this ...
you see ... hmm ... uh-huh
... yeah ... I mean ... let's
say ... right ... um ... um
... well ... now ... er ...
ah ... well ... it's ... um
... er ... ah ... now ...

er ... ah ... well ... you
see ... hmm ... uh-huh ...
yeah ... right ... right ...
okay ... here goes ... um

... will you excuse me for
a moment, readers? I'll
be right back.

'What's going on, Terry?' says Jill. 'Why has the story stopped?'

'Don't you mean, why hasn't it *started*?' I say.

'Well, that's the thing,' says Terry. 'I'm not sure how to start. Can you help me, Andy?'

'You could try starting with *Once upon a time*,'
I say. 'That's good for beginners.'

'Thanks!' says Terry. 'You're a real pal, Pal.
You're a pally pal. A real pally wally—'

'All right, just get on with it,' I say. 'The readers
are getting impatient. It's the end of the second
chapter and the story hasn't even begun!'

'Relax, Andy,' says Terry. 'I'll get it started
right away.'

CHAPTER 3

# TERRY'S DUMB DOT STORY
## (Part One)

Once upon
a time
there was
a ... dot.

And the
dot was all
alone ...

but then
along
came
another
dot ...

so then
there
were
TWO
dots!

And the dots fell in love ...

and had baby dots.

Soon there were
LOTS OF DOTS!

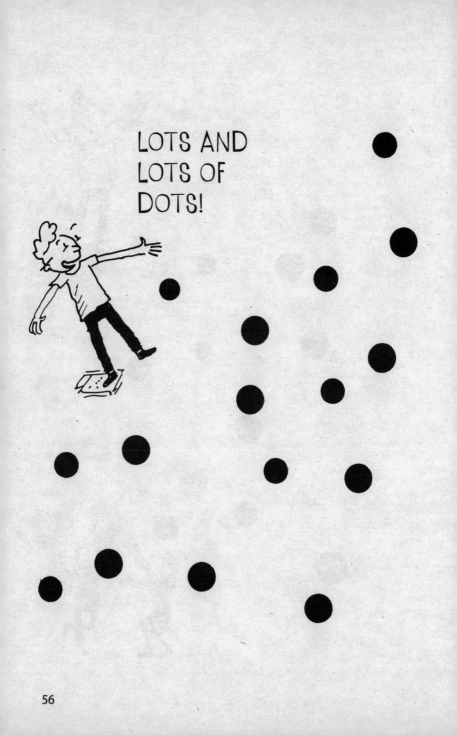

LOTS AND
LOTS OF
DOTS!

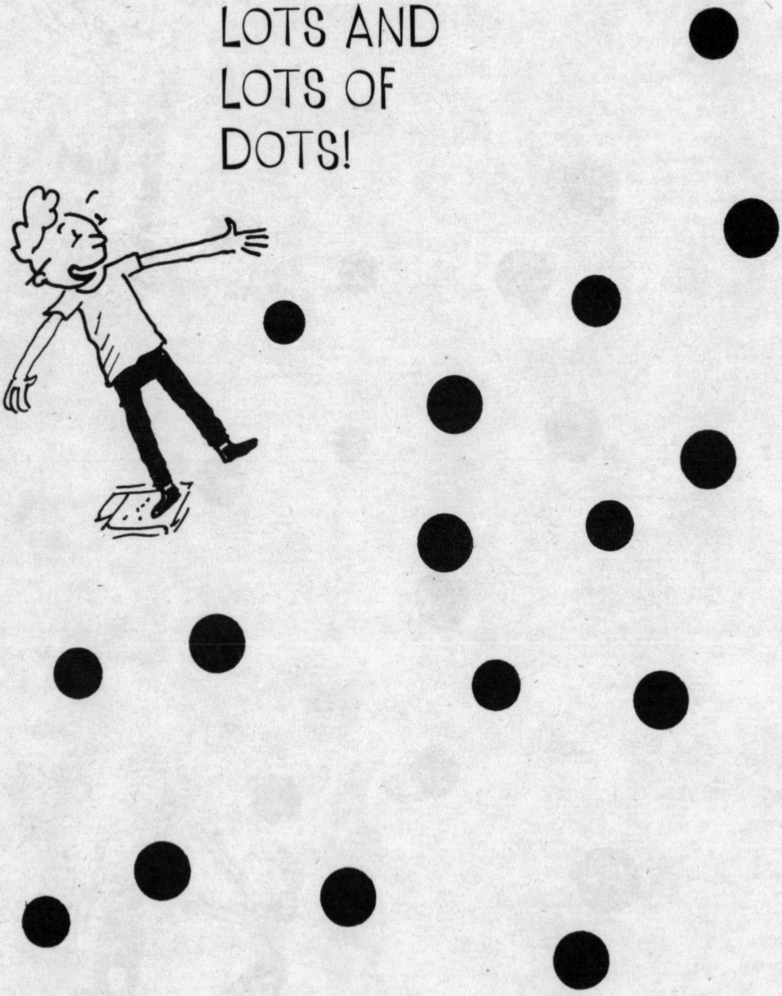

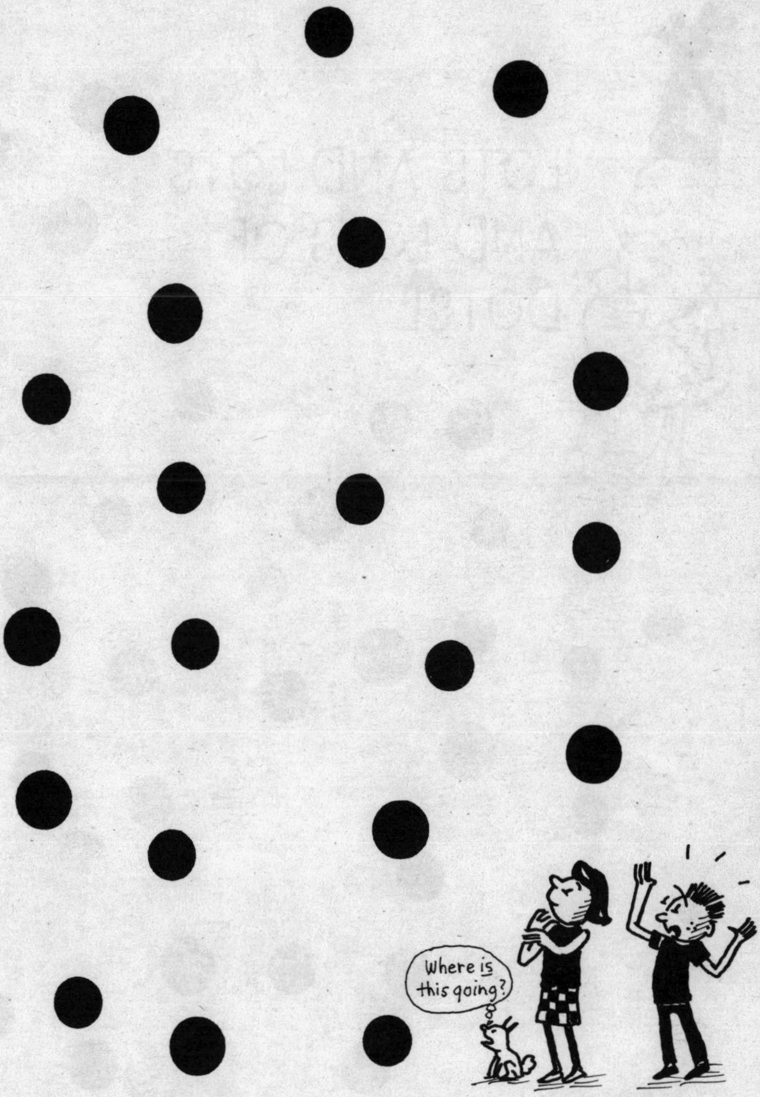
Where is this going?

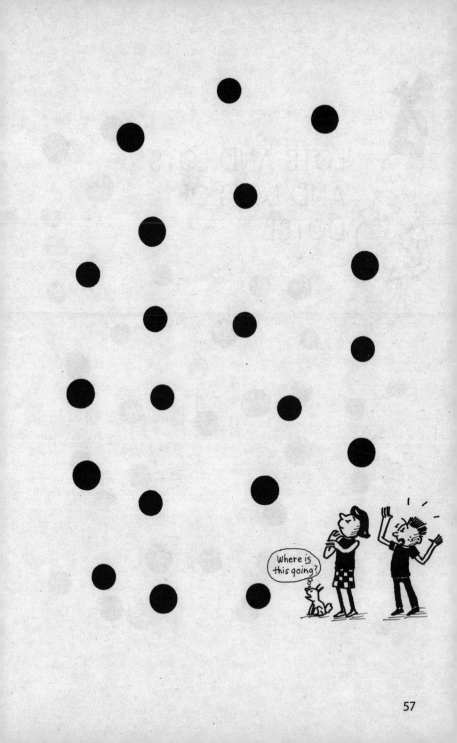

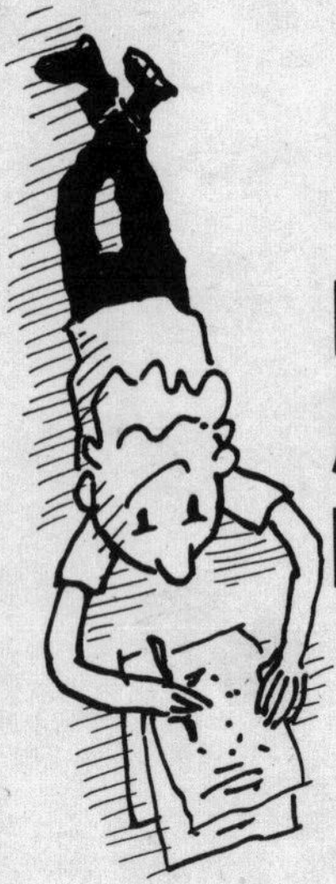

# LOTS AND LOTS AND LOTS OF DOTS!

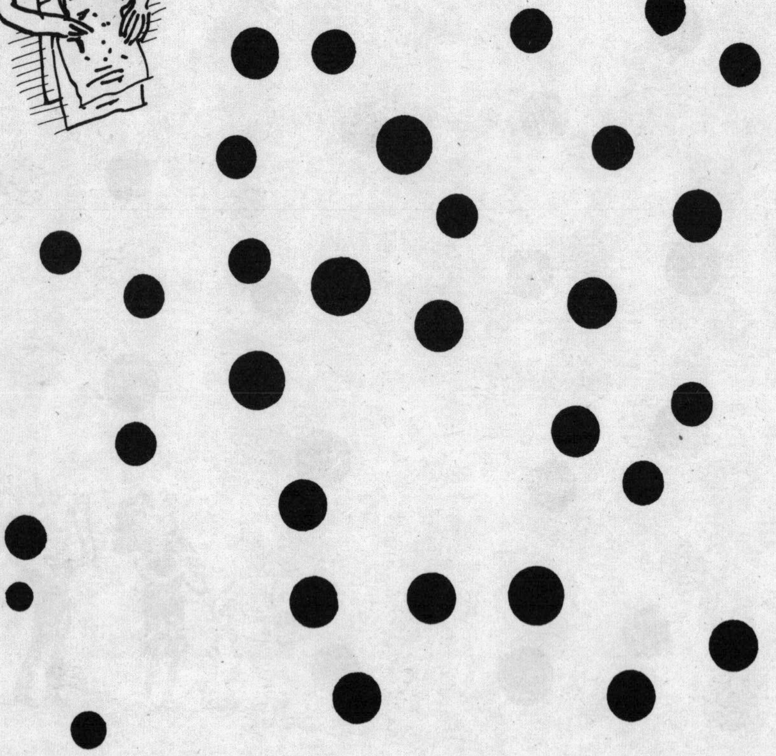

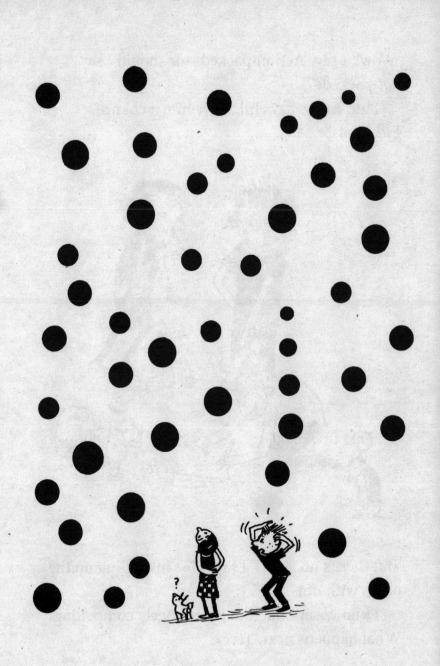

'Wow!' I say. 'Action-packed—or should I say *dot*-packed?'

'Shh, Andy,' says Jill. 'Give him a chance. I *like* dots!'

'But there's no story!' I say. 'He's just filling up the pages with dots.'

'I know,' says Jill, 'but it's strangely compelling. What happens next, Terry?'

Well, um, er, then the dots starting joining up and turning into lines.

Soon there were lots
of lines!

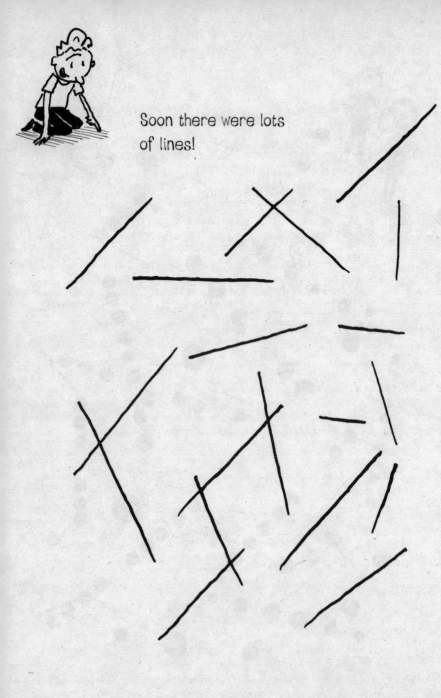

# LOTS AND LOTS OF LINES!

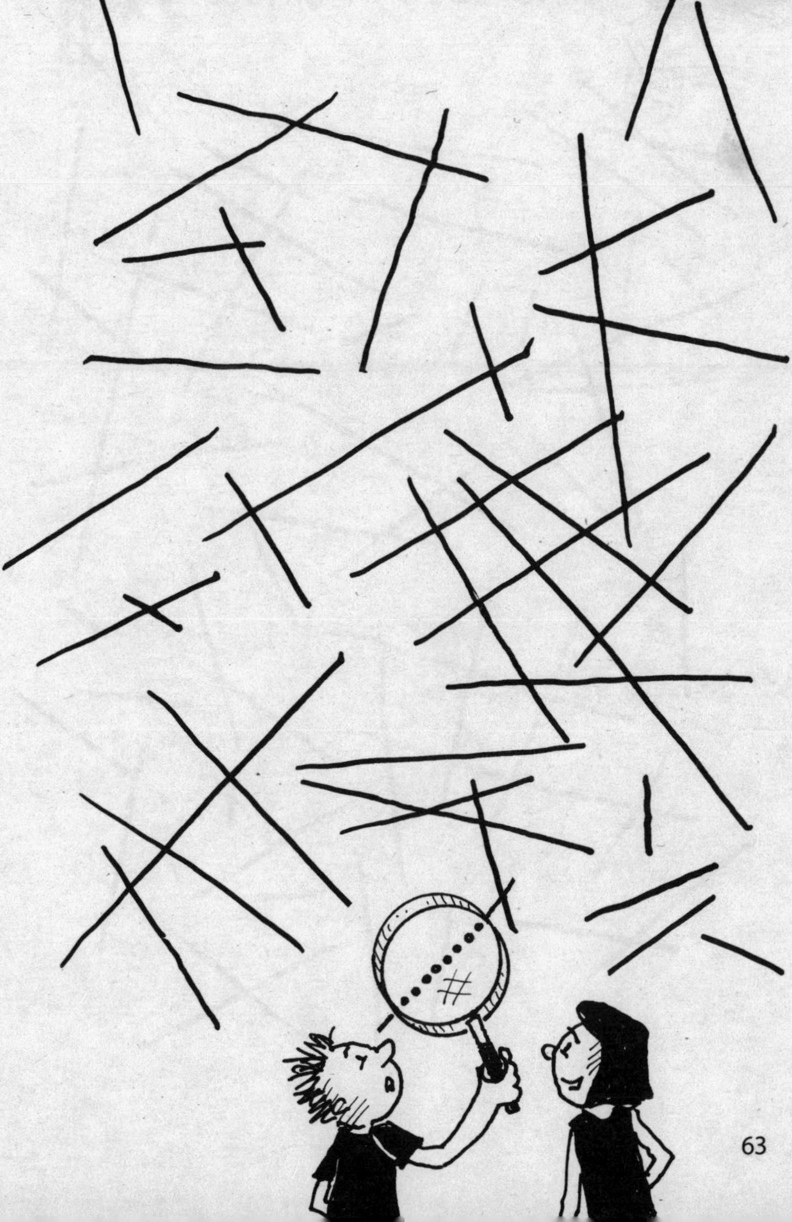

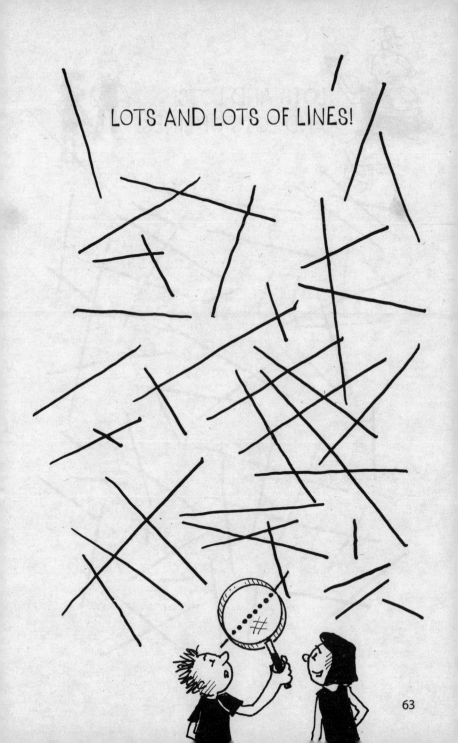

LOTS AND LOTS
AND LOTS OF LINES!

And then the lines started curving and bending ...

and joining up
to make ... shapes!

# LOTS OF SHAPES!

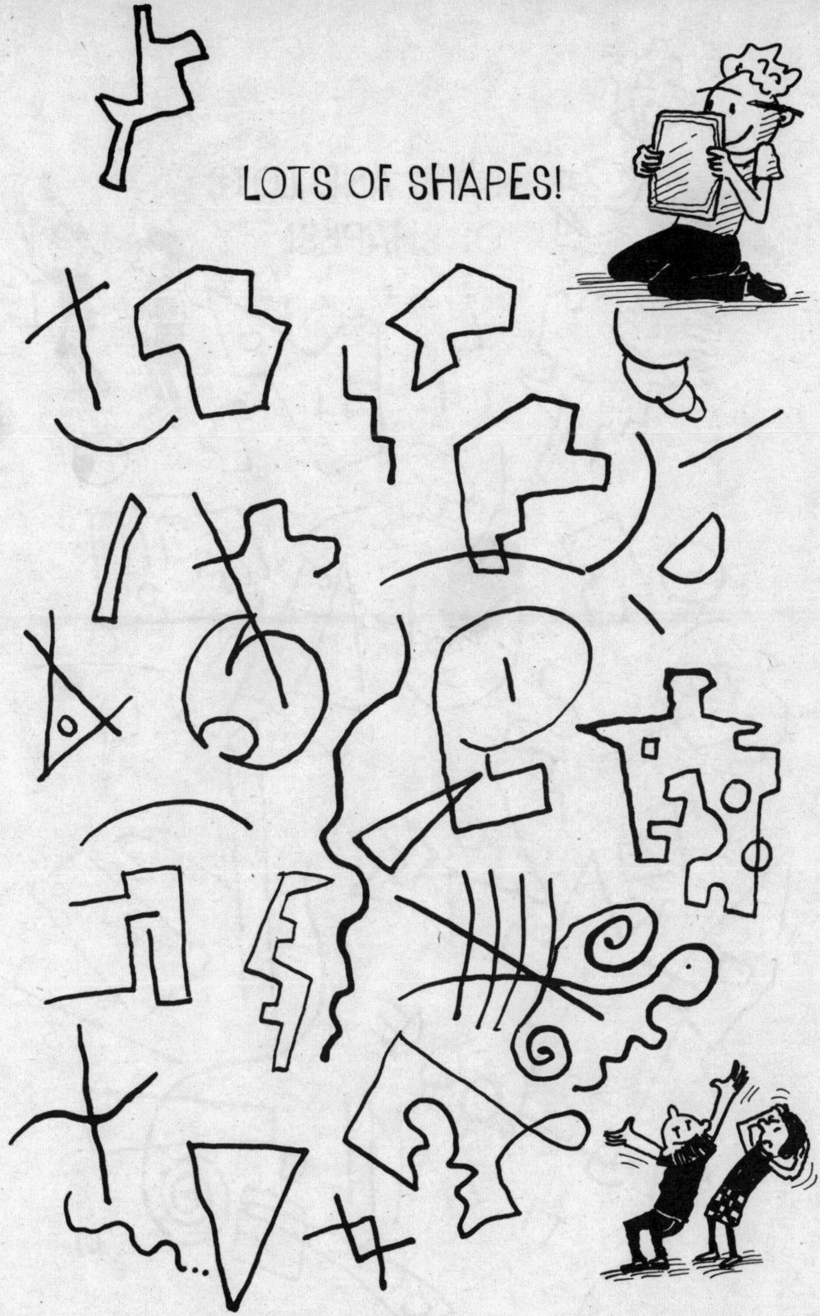

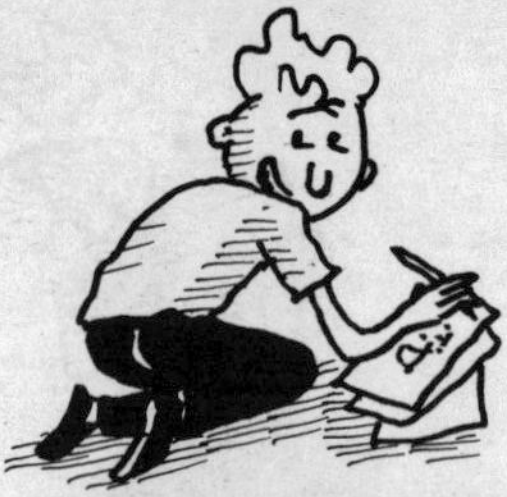

# LOTS AND LOTS OF SHAPES!

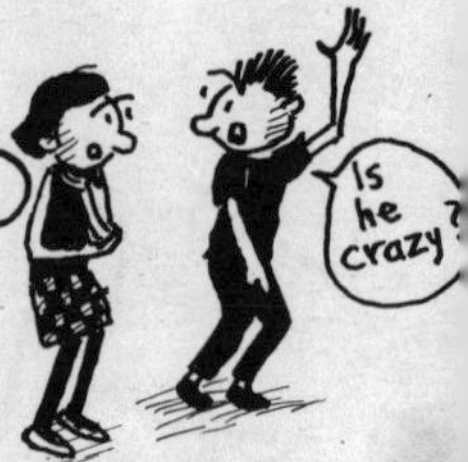
Is he crazy?

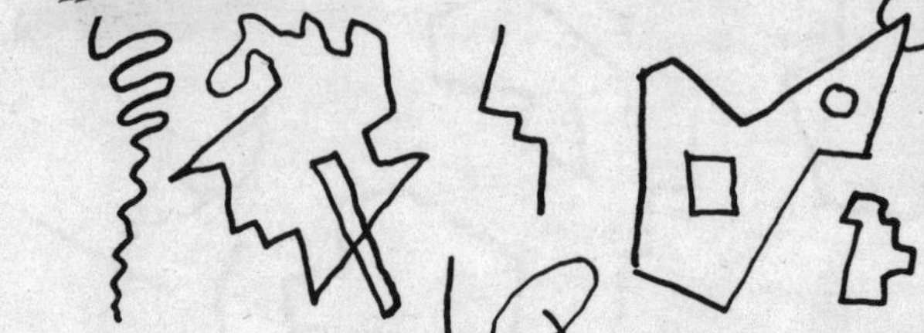

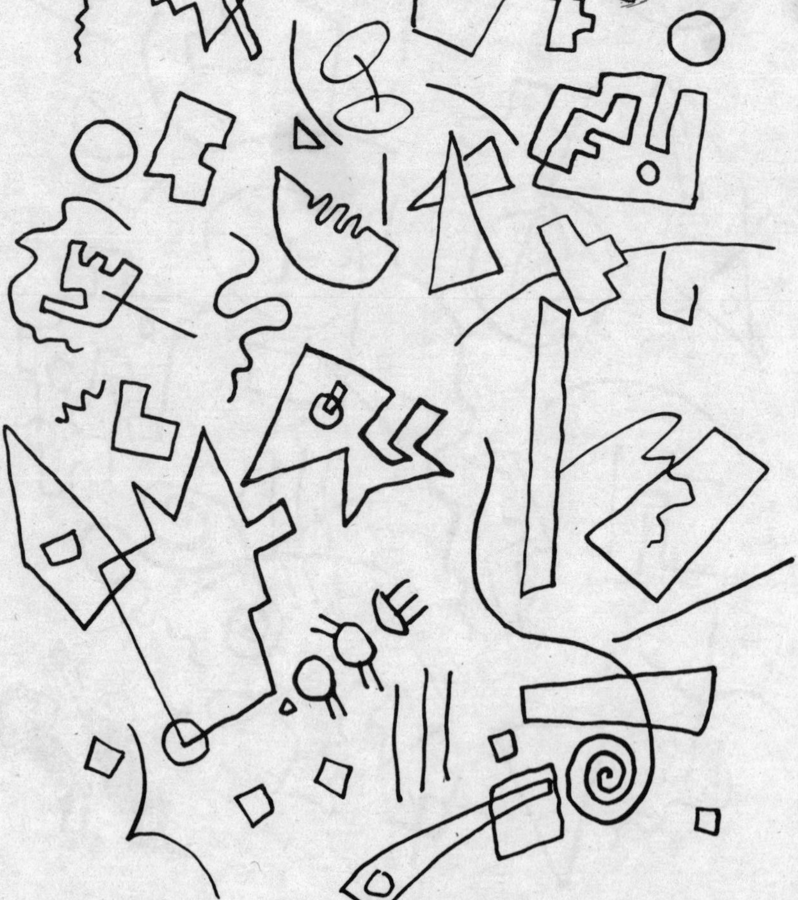

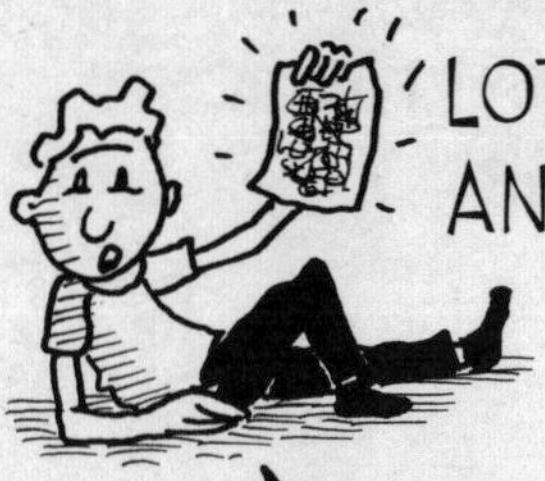

# LOTS AND LOTS AND LOTS OF SHAPES!

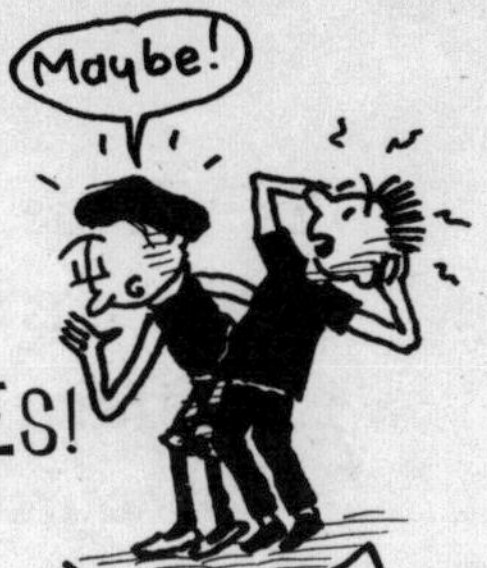
Maybe!

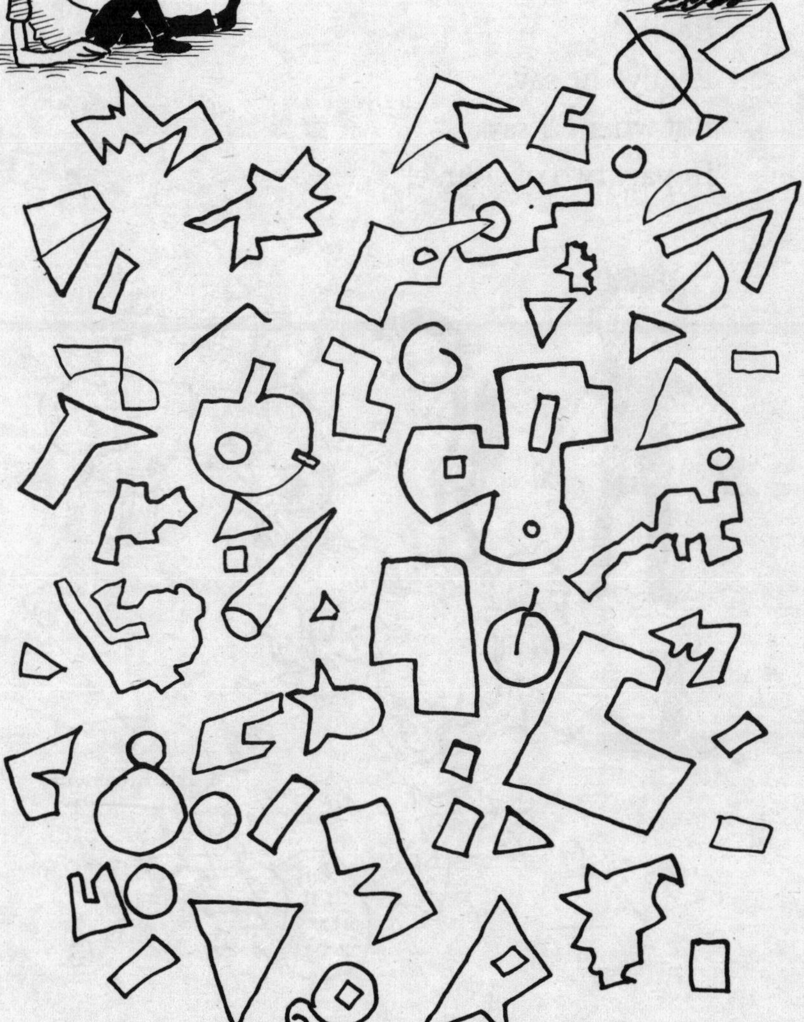

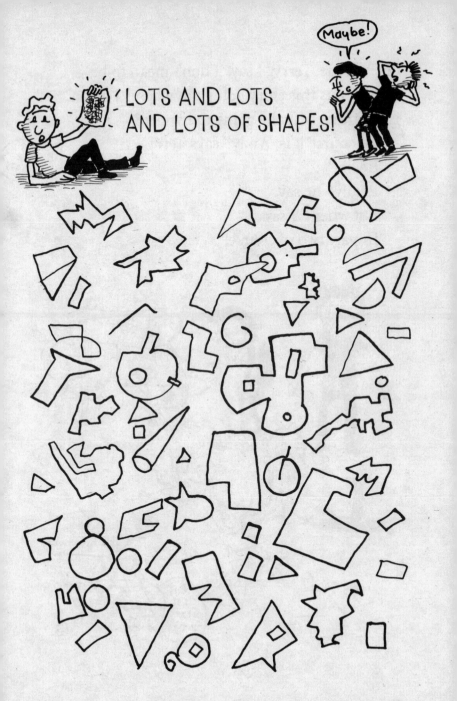

'Excuse me, Terry,' I say, 'I don't mean to be rude, but is this story going anywhere? I mean, is anything actually going to happen?'

'Of course it is, Andy!' says Terry.

'Really?'

'Really!' he says.

'But when?' I say.

'In part two of course!'

CHAPTER 4

# TERRY'S DUMB DOT STORY (Part Two)

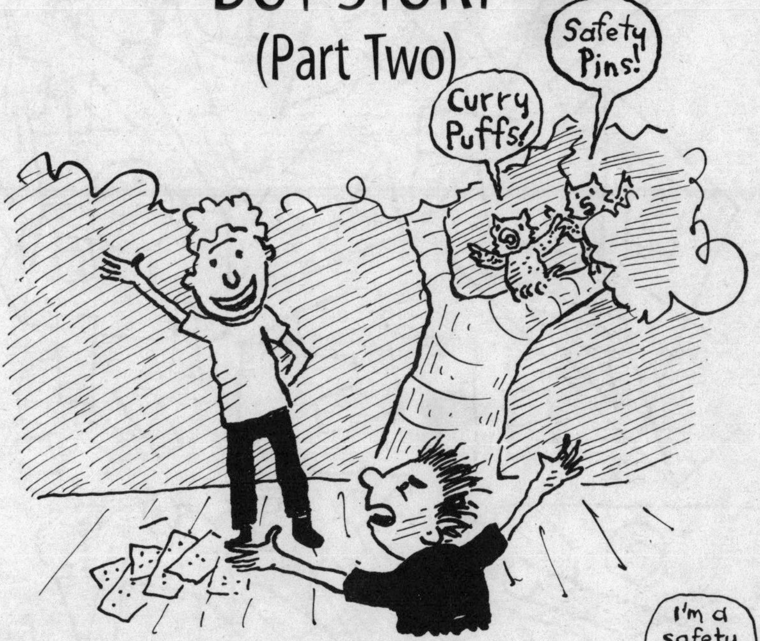
Curry Puffs!
Safety Pins!

Hi, my name's Terry. Welcome to part two of my exciting story.

If you're like most of my readers—

'Get on with it!' I say.

'Okay,' says Terry.

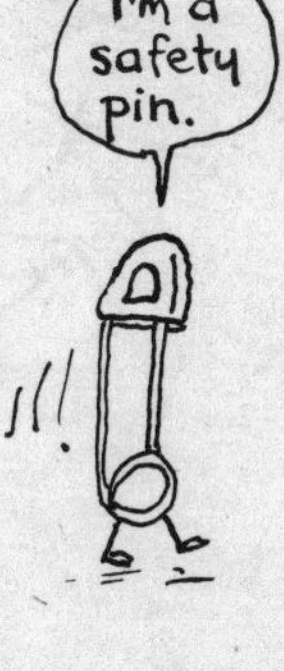
I'm a safety pin.

Well, it wasn't long before the shapes started joining up and becoming more complicated shapes—like this …

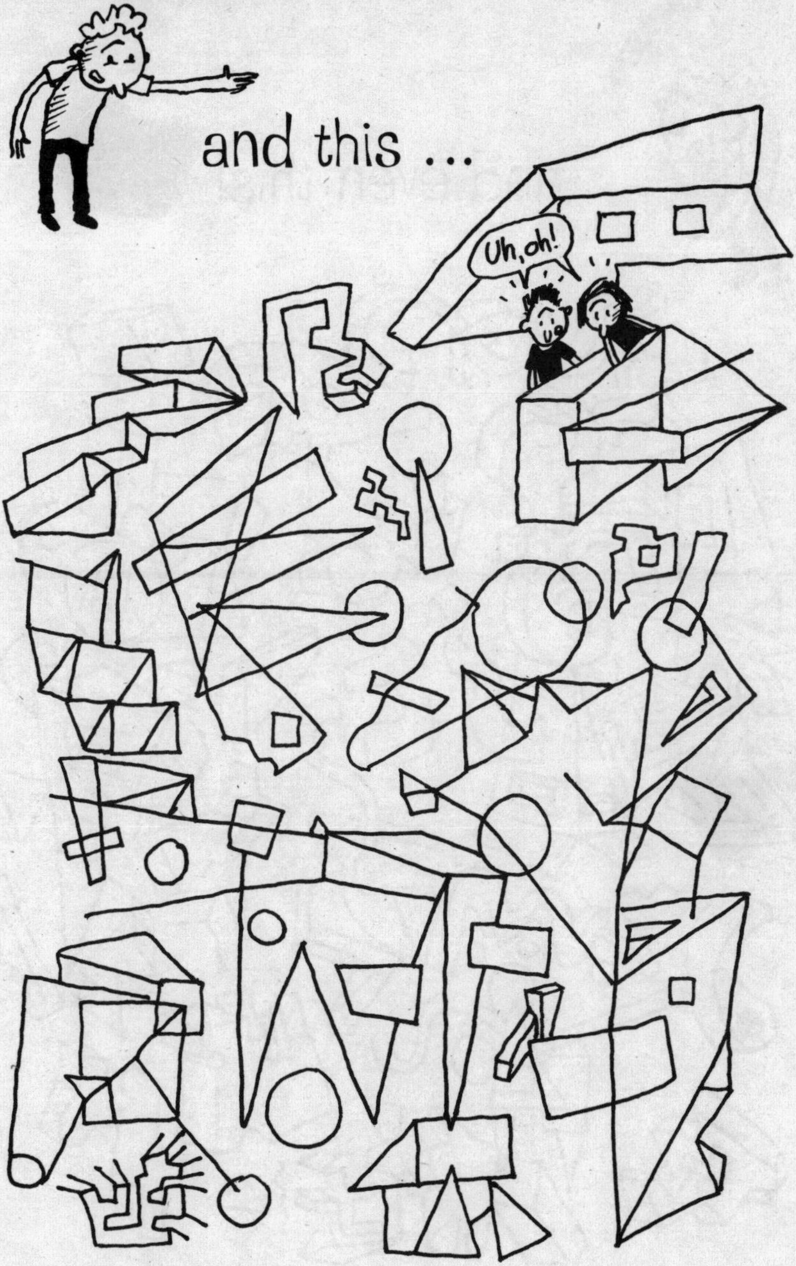
and this ...
Uh, oh!

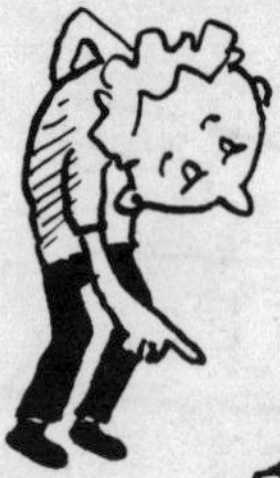

and even this!

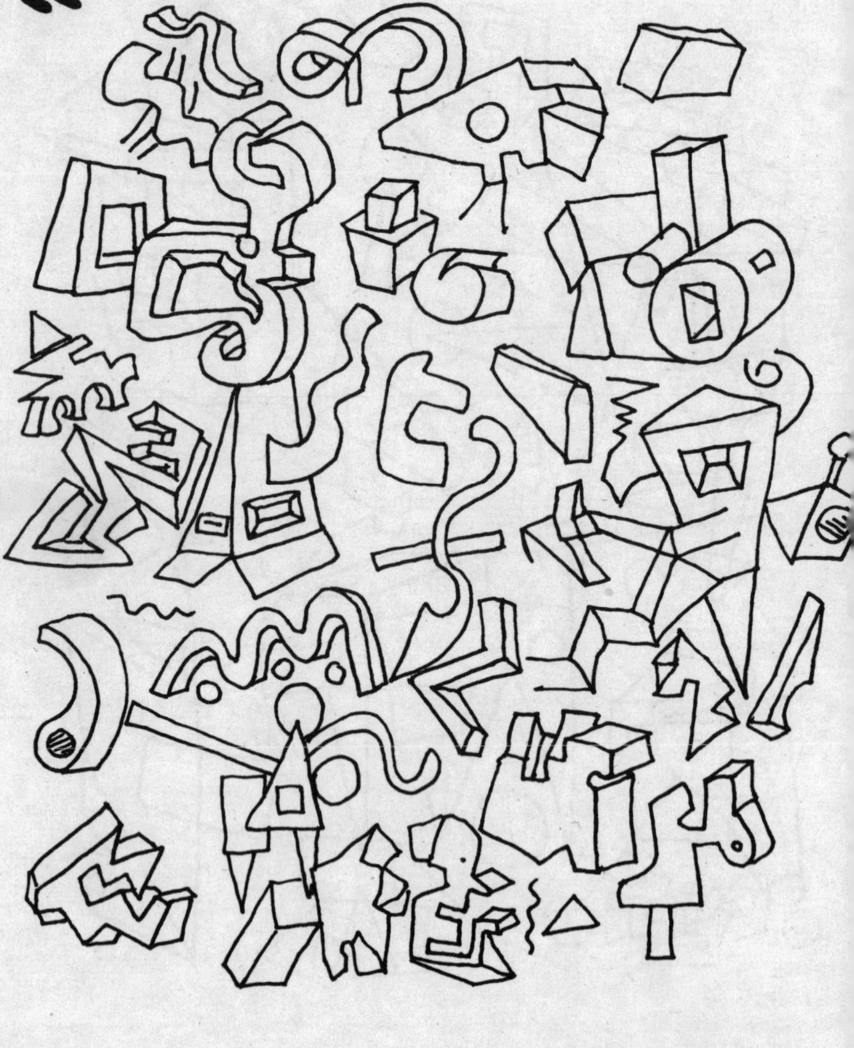

But once they started they couldn't stop. The shapes just kept multiplying ...

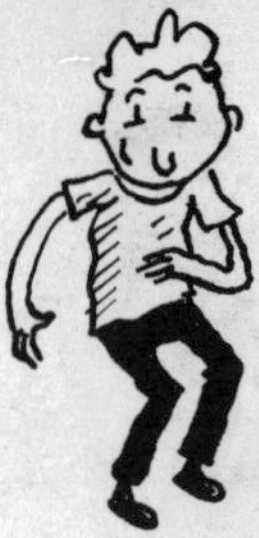

and multiplying ...

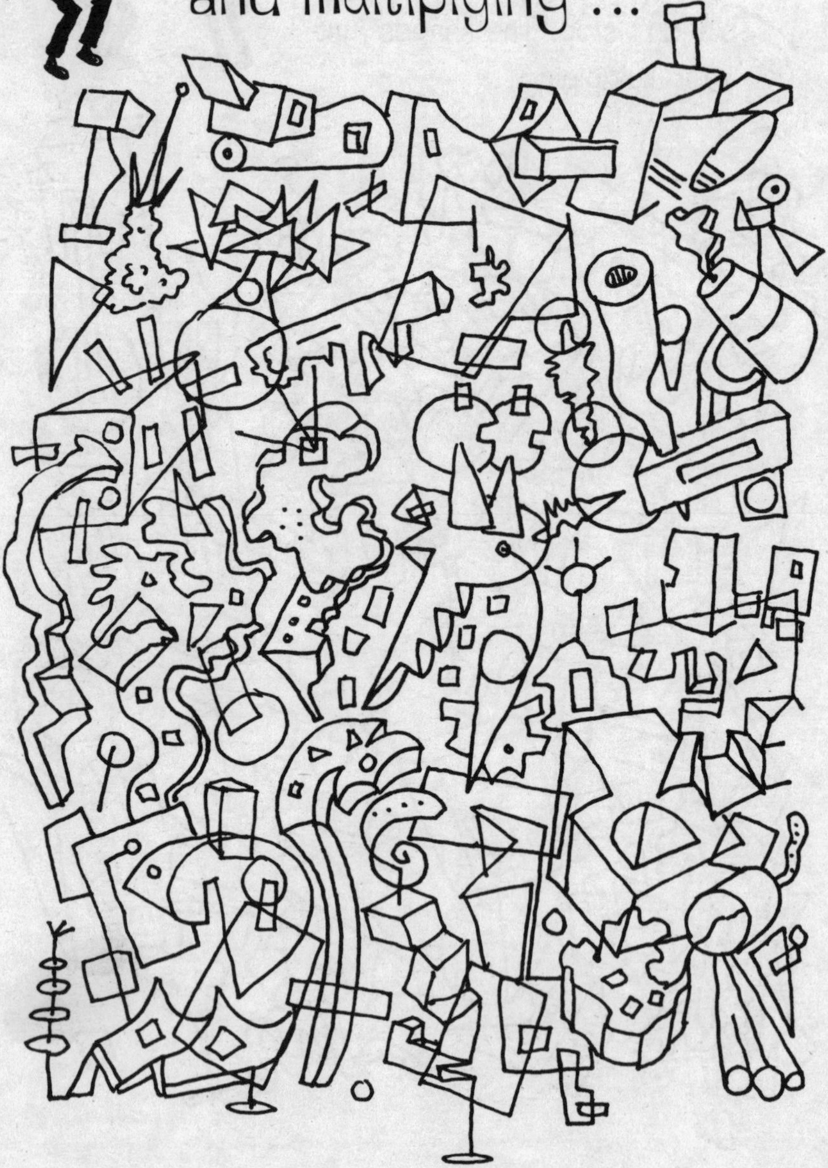

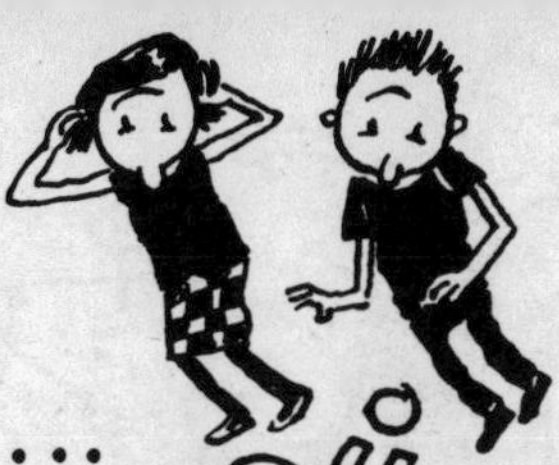

and multiplying ...

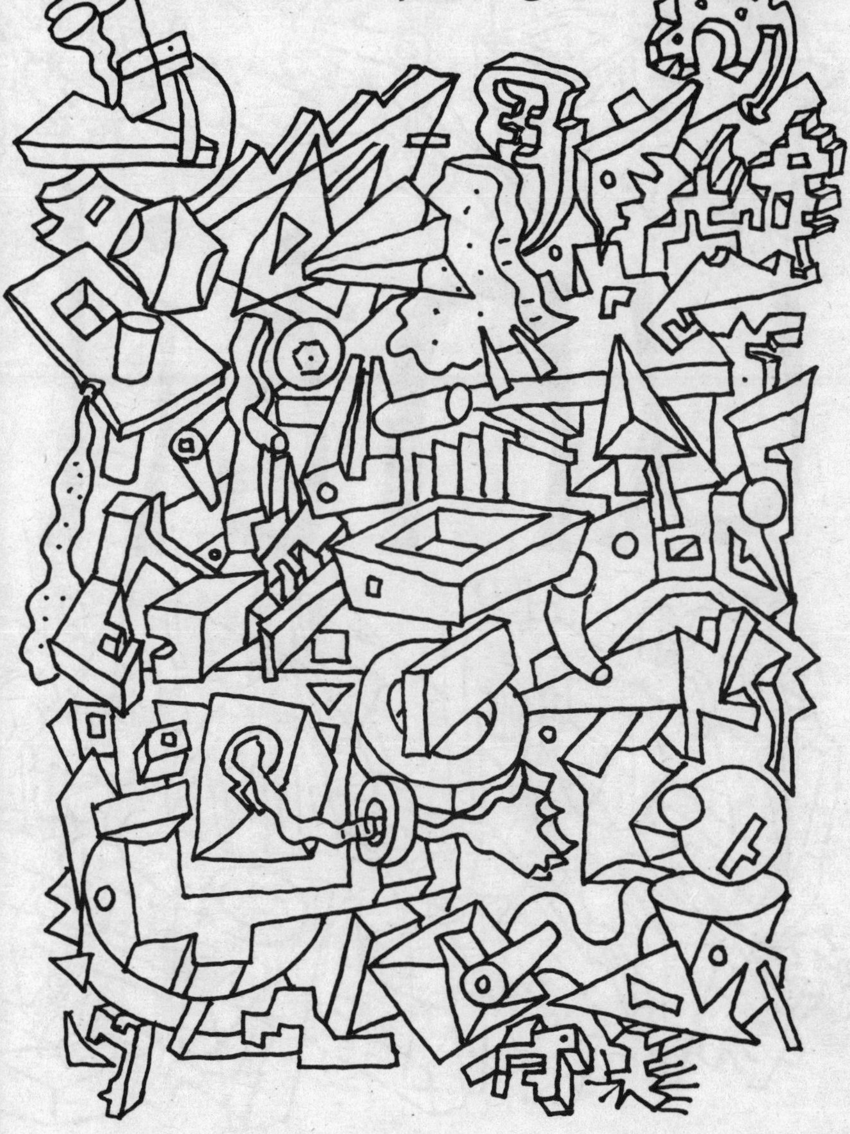

# until

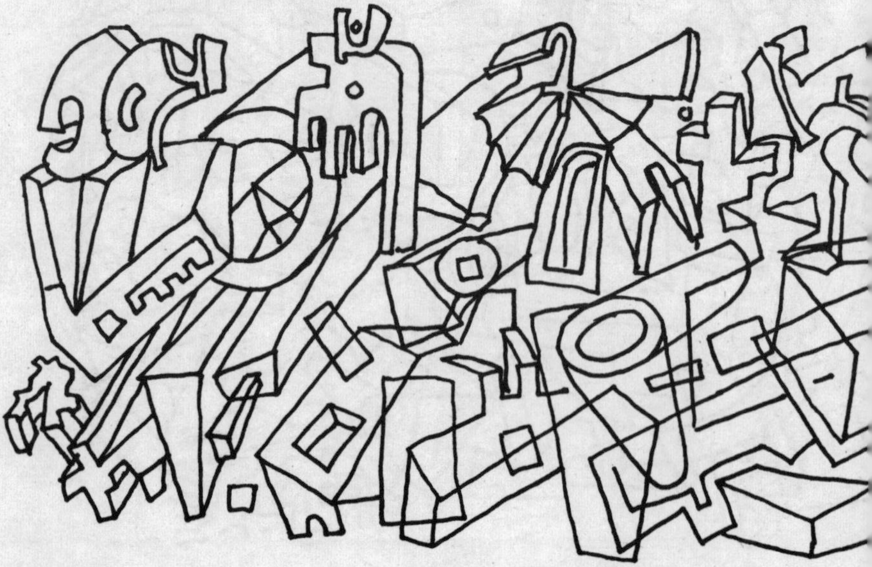

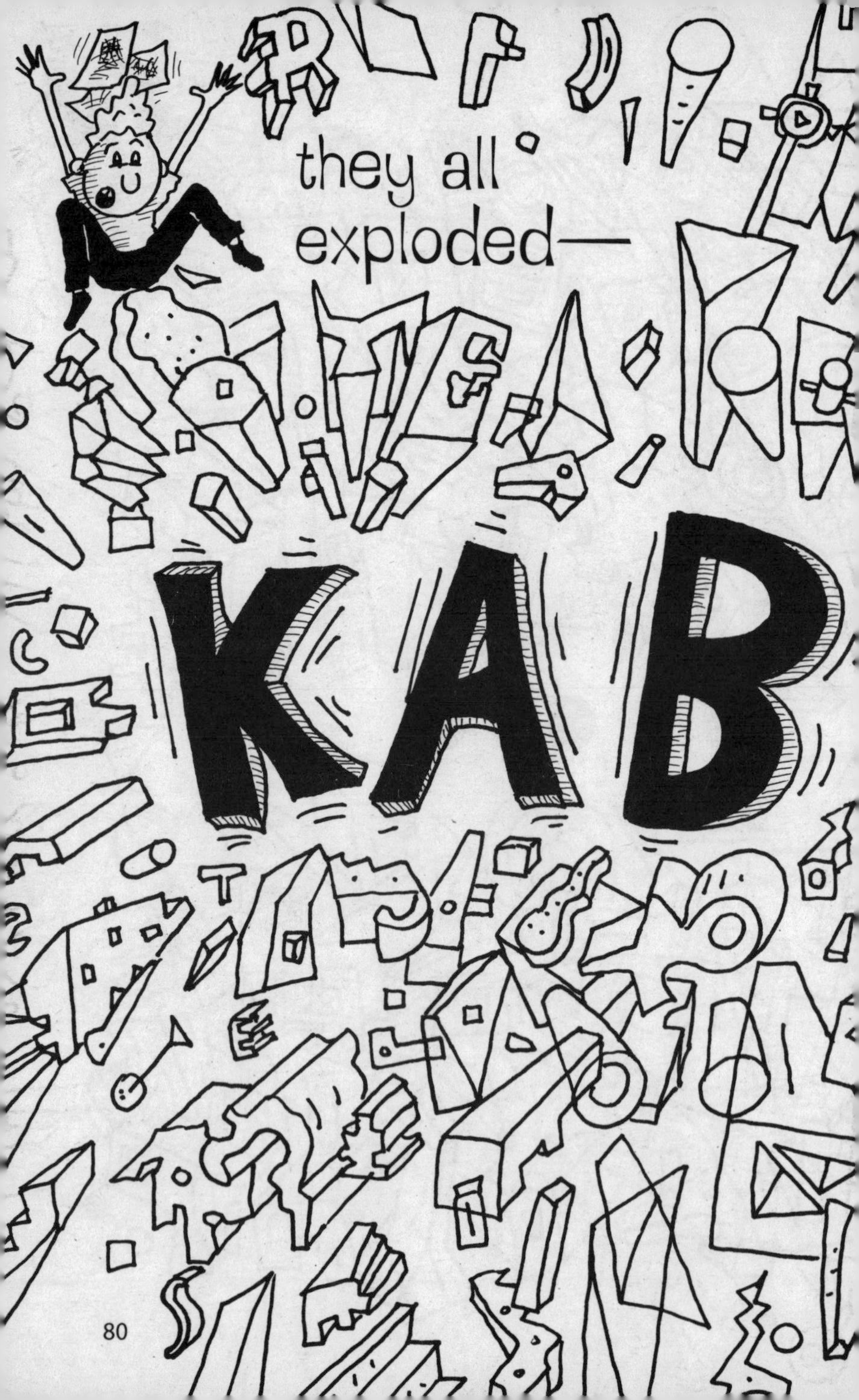
they all exploded—
KAB

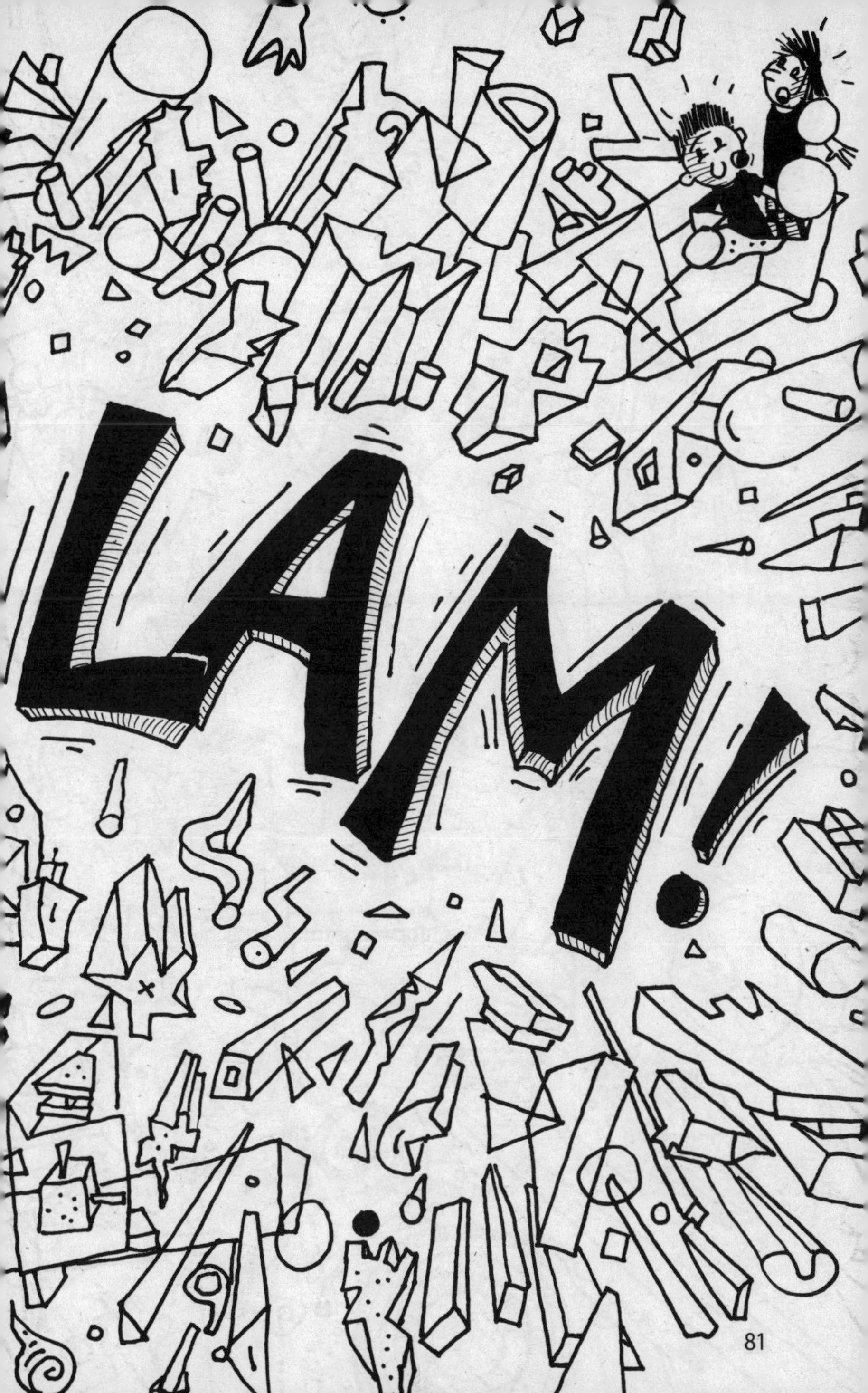
LAM!

'Uh-oh,' says Terry.

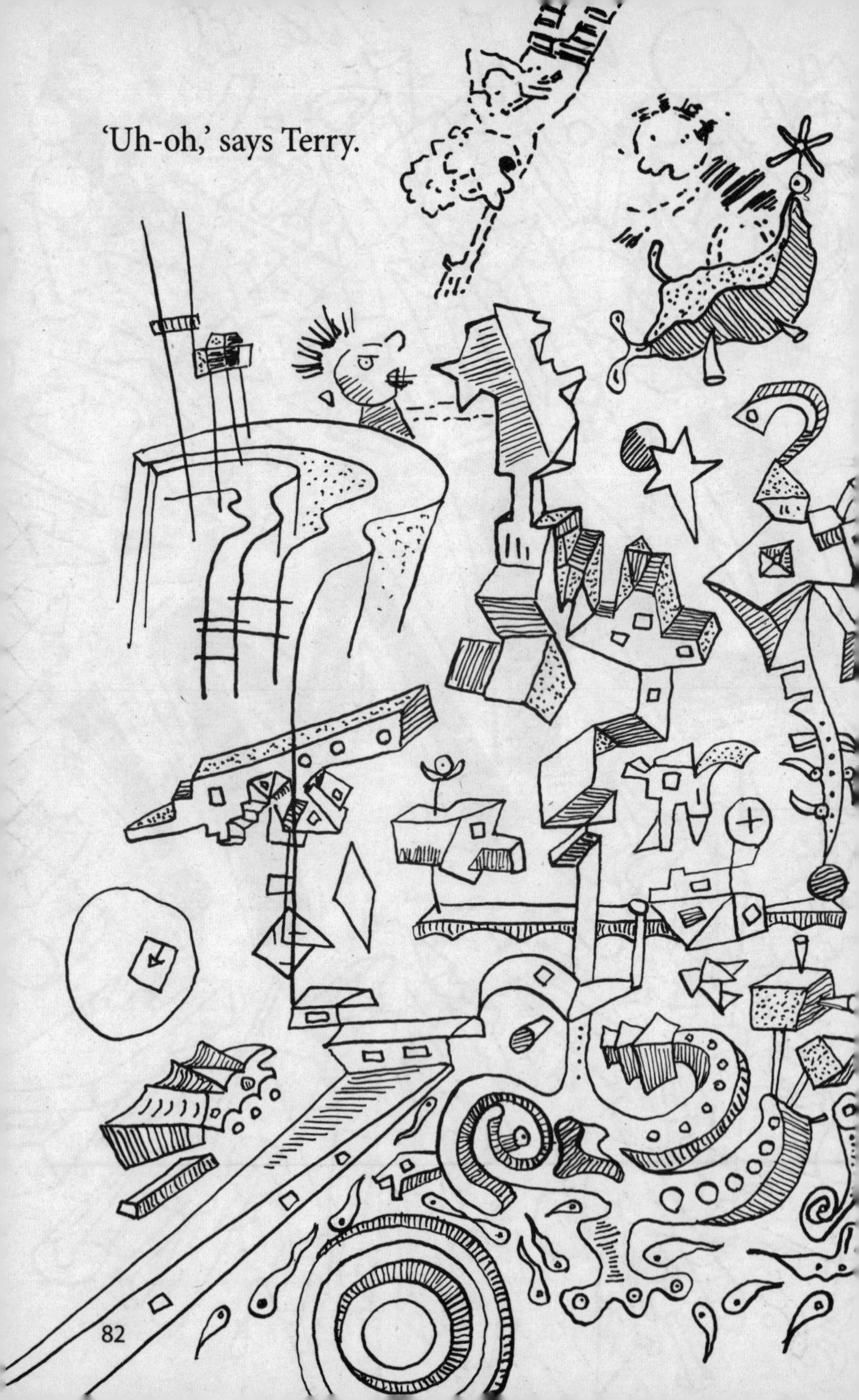

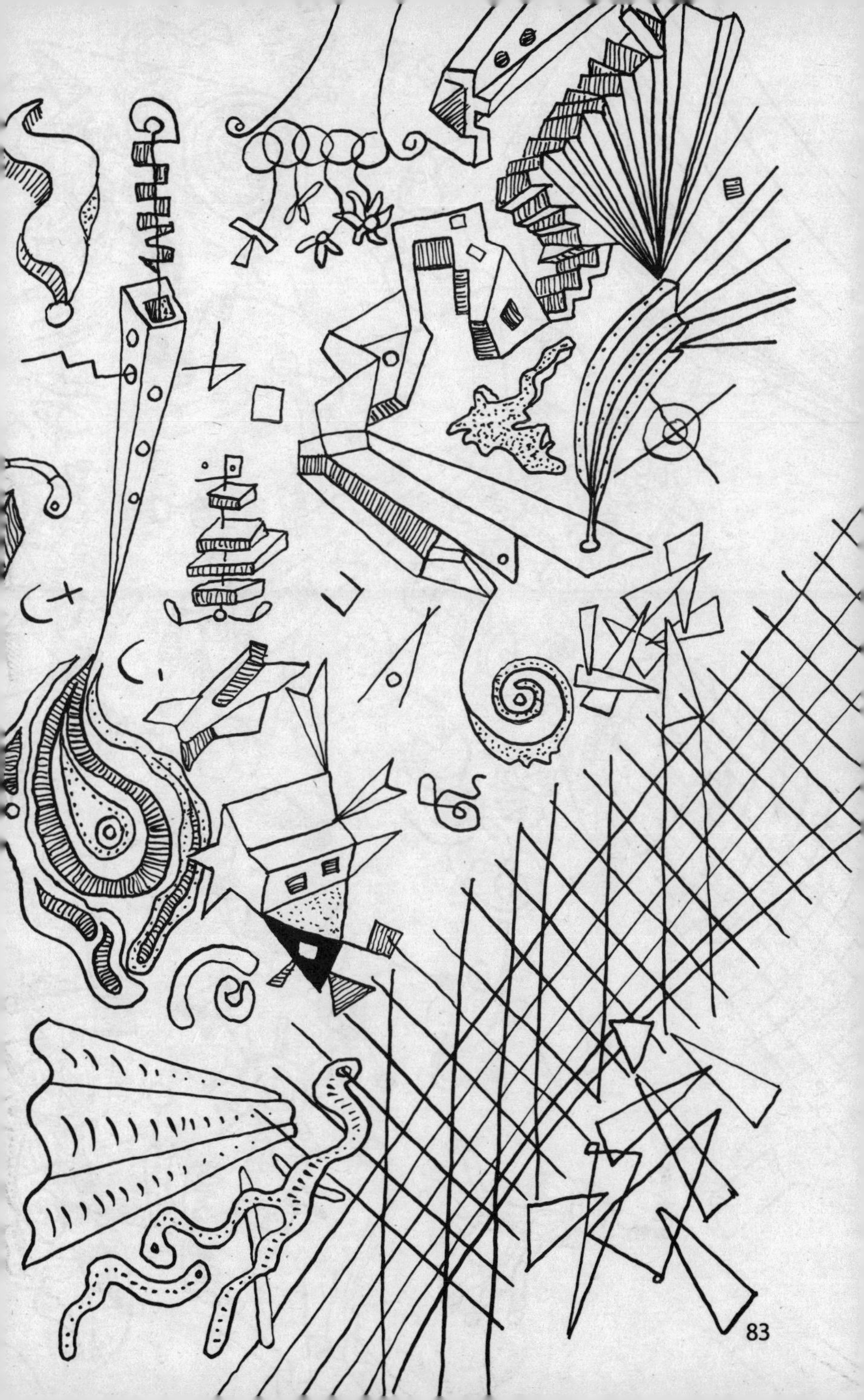

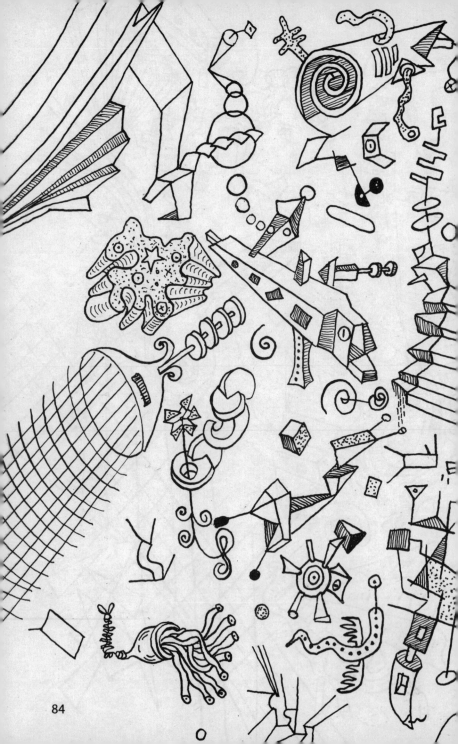

'What happened?' says Jill. 'Why has everything gone so weird? I feel strange.'

'You *look* strange,' I say.

'So do you,' says Jill.

'Oh, no!' I say, looking down at my body, which is now just a collection of random shapes. 'What have you done, Terry?'

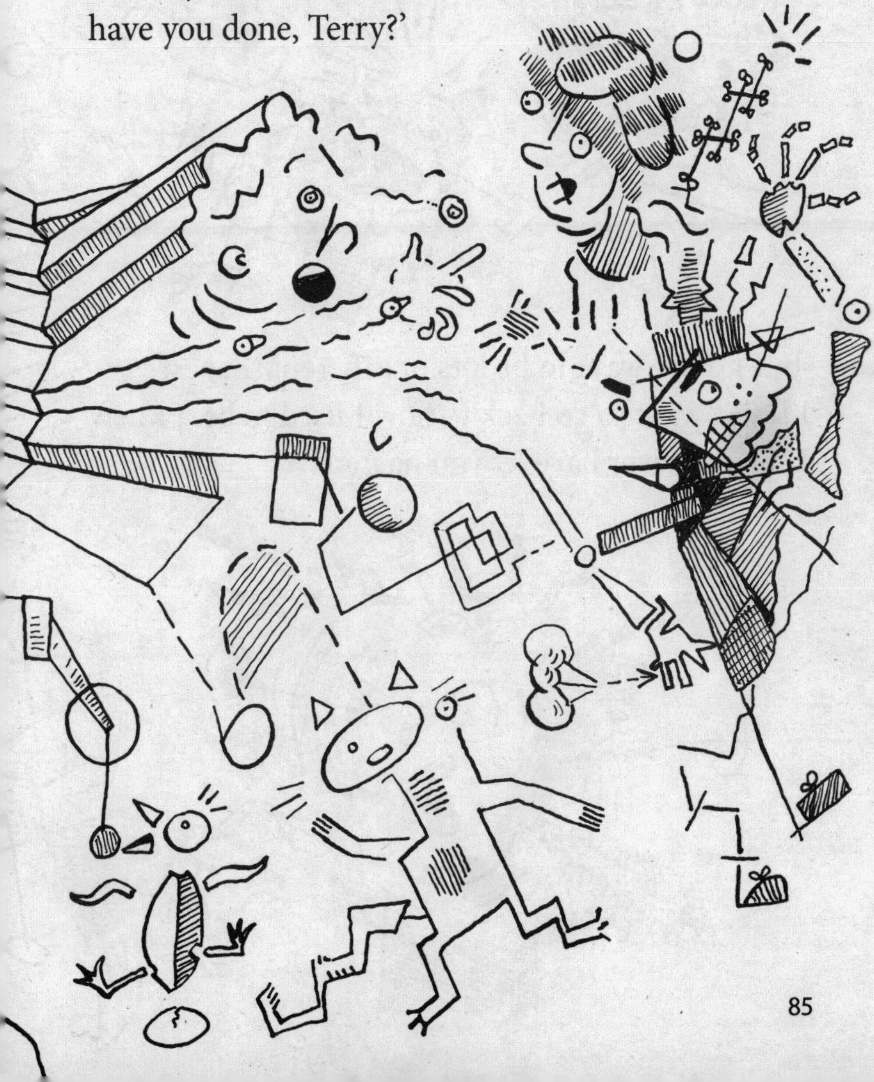

'I haven't *done* anything,' he says. 'You already were a collection of shapes that together formed the shape of a human being! You're still you, just in a different shape—well, *lots* of different shapes.'

'But I don't want to be lots of different shapes!' I say. 'I want to go back to how I used to be. I knew I should never have let you narrate!'

'Don't be too hard on him, Andy,' says Jill. 'The story isn't over yet. What happens next, Terry?'

'Um … er … ah … um …' says Terry. 'I don't know.'

'Well, that's just great!' I say.

Jill turns to me. 'What do you think should happen, Andy?'

'How should I know?' I say. 'It's Terry's dumb dot story, not mine.'

'Well somebody has to do *something*,' says Jill.
'Look at my animals! They've gone all weird too!
This is like a dream—a really bad dream!'

'That's it, Jill!' I say.
  'What's it?' says Jill.

'*It's a dream* is the key to ending this story,'
I say. 'It's not the *best* way to end a story but
sometimes—if you're really stuck—it's the only
thing you can do, and this *is* an emergency.'

I clear my throat and start narrating as fast as
I can:

And then, suddenly, we all woke up and realised it
was all just a dream—a really DUMB dream!

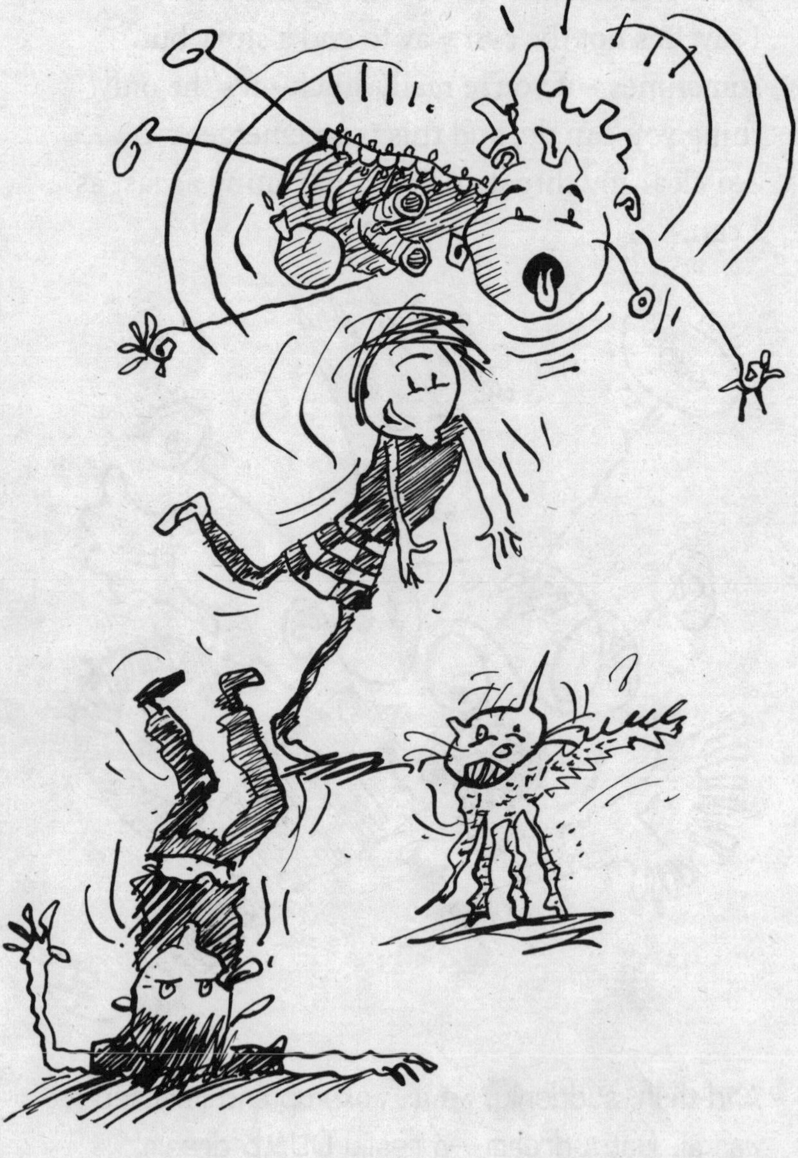

'You did it!' says Jill. 'We're back to normal!'

'Yes,' I say, 'but I couldn't have done it without you. You gave me the idea.'

'And you couldn't have done it without me either!' says Terry. 'It was my dots that started it.'

'Yes,' I say, 'but it was my ending that finished it and saved us all.'

'Actually, I'm not so sure about that,' says Jill.

'Why not?' I say.

'Look,' she says, pointing to the ground below, 'it's the Story Police—they *are* real!'

'That's what I tried to tell you,' I say.

'Yikes!' says Terry.

'OPEN UP!' calls a loud voice. 'It's the Story Police here. We've had reports of a dumb dot story with an illegal *it-was-all-just-a-dream* ending coming from this treehouse and you are our chief suspects. There is no use resisting. We have your tree surrounded!'

'What do we do now?' says Terry.

'Open the door and let them in,' says Jill. 'I'm sure they'll understand if we just explain what happened.'

'No,' I say. 'That's not going to work. This isn't the normal police. This is the *Story Police*—they are *really* strict. We have to come up with a different ending ... or else!'

'Any ideas?' says Terry.

'Yes,' I say. 'RUN!'

## CHAPTER 5

# RUN! RIDE!

So
we
run.

We run up.

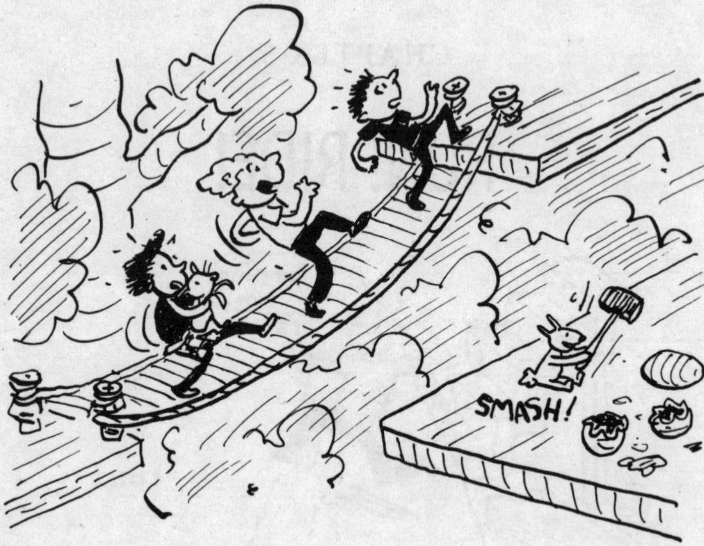
SMASH!

We run down.

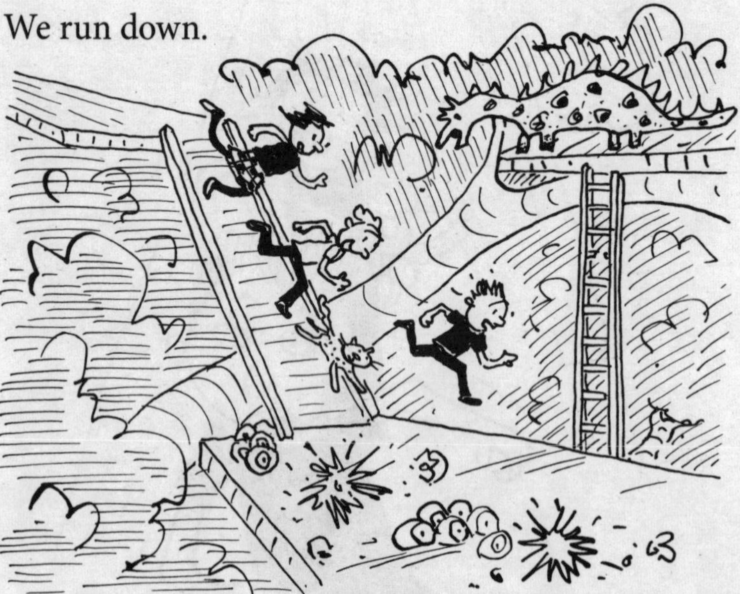

We run straight.

We run around.

Around …

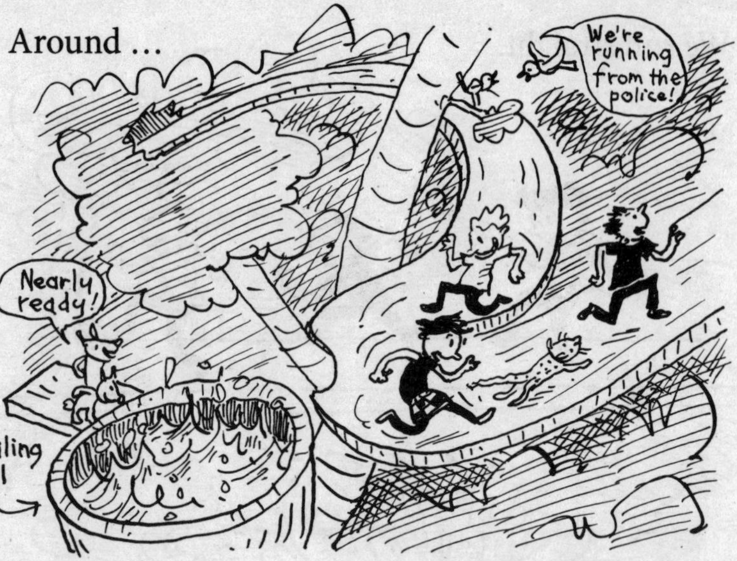
We're running from the police!
Nearly ready!
Boiling oil

and around …

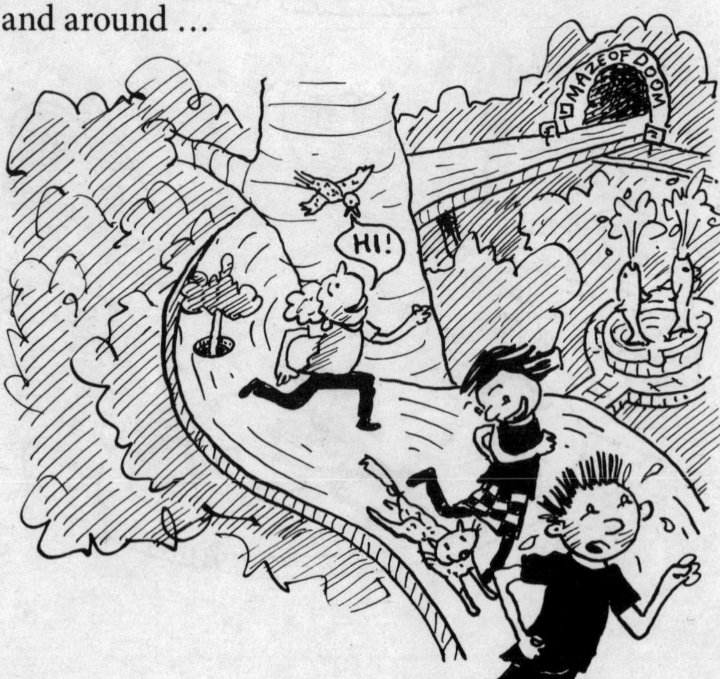
MAZE OF DOOM
HI!

and around …

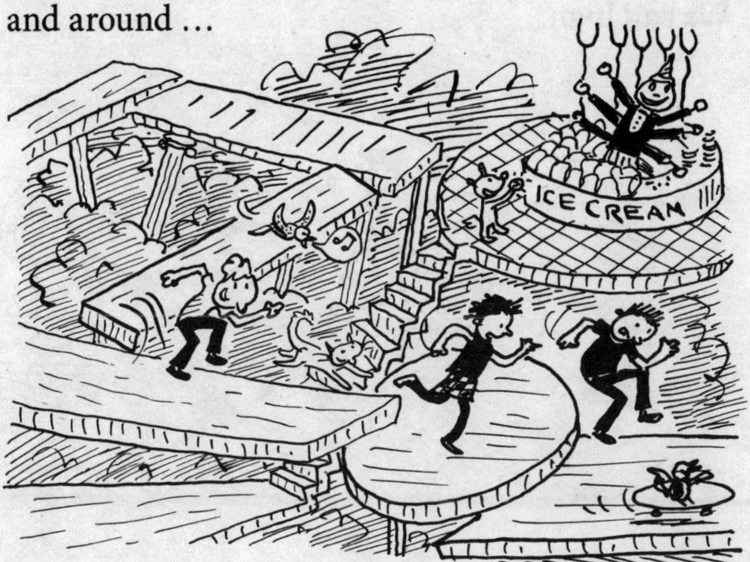
ICE CREAM

and around.

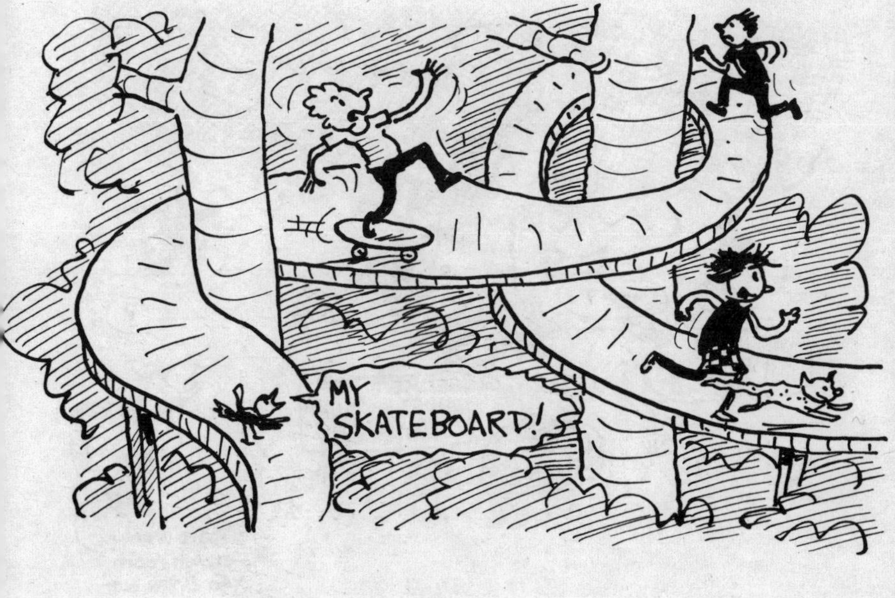
MY SKATEBOARD!

We run high.

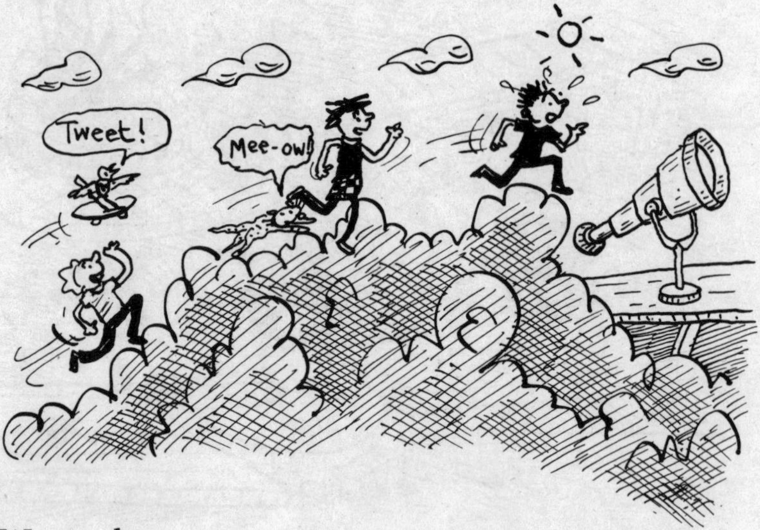
Tweet!
Mee-ow!

We run low.

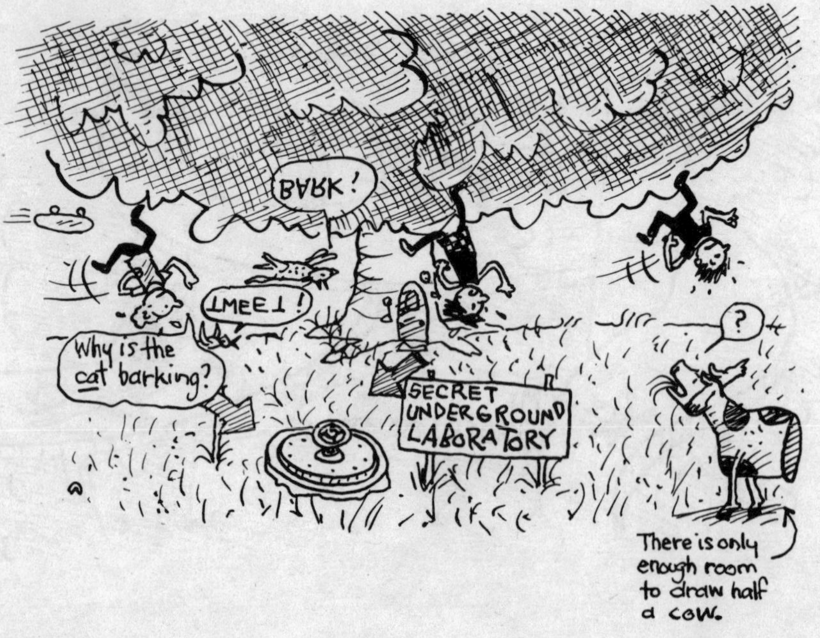
BARK!
TWEET!
Why is the cat barking?
SECRET UNDERGROUND LABORATORY
?
There is only enough room to draw half a cow.

We run fast.

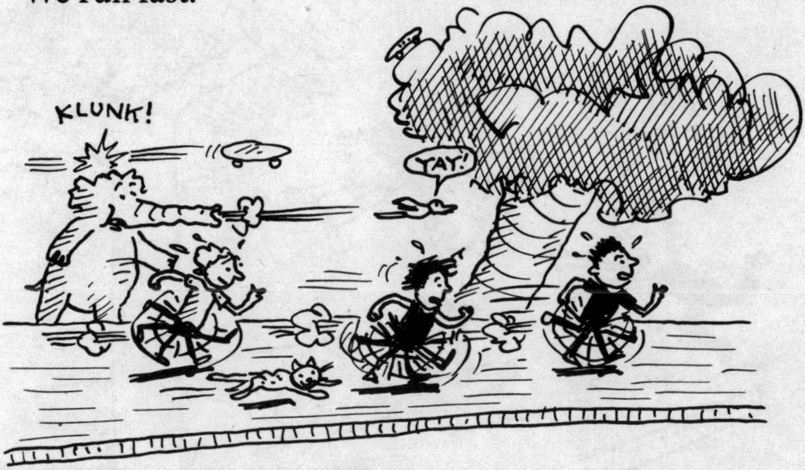
KLUNK!
YAY!

We run slow.

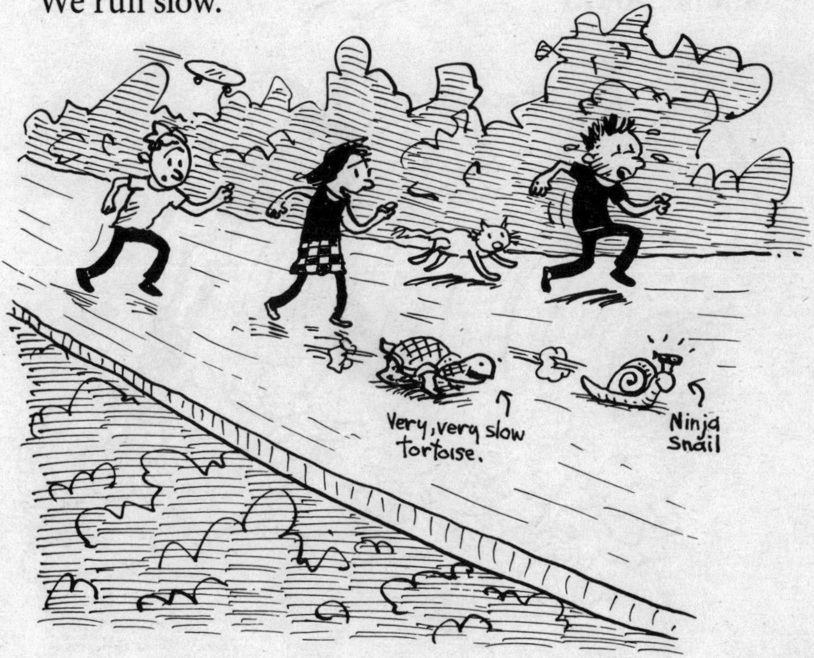
Very, very slow tortoise.
Ninja Snail

We go …

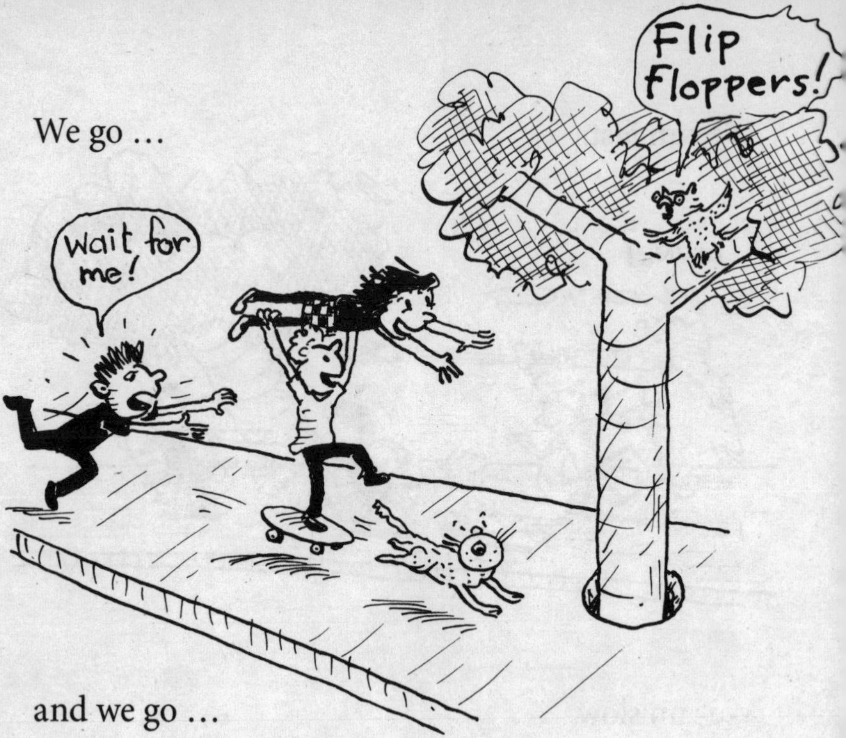
Flip Floppers!
Wait for me!

and we go …

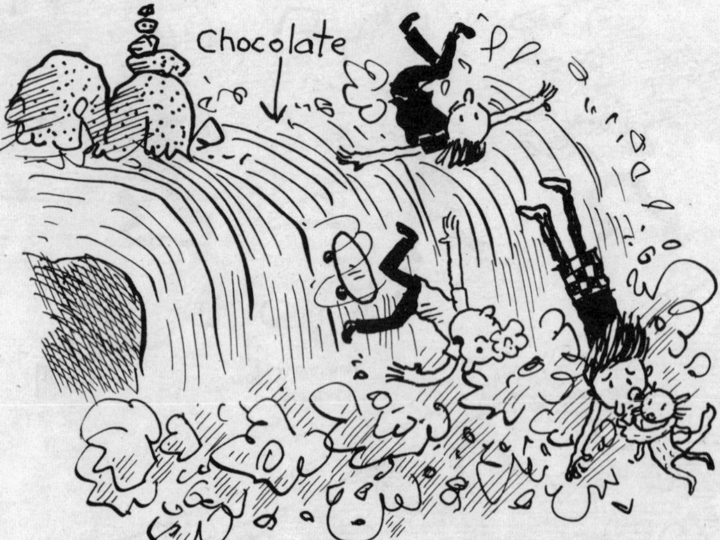
Chocolate

and we go …

BOING!

BOUNCE!

Word

Cat

Bouncy
thing.

and we go…

GASP!

sweat

red face

'STOP!' says Terry, bent over and puffing. 'I need a rest!'

'We have to keep going,' I say. 'The Story Police are right behind us.'

'In here!' says Jill, opening the gate to the tiny-horse paddock. 'Quick—but be careful you don't step on any of the tiny horses!'

PUFF! PANT!

sweat ↑

We tiptoe in.

The tiny horses gallop up to us.

'They're *so* cute,' says Terry. 'I wish they were big enough to ride.'

'They can be,' says Jill. 'Watch this.'

She whinnies quietly and the tiny horses group together ...

and assemble themselves into a regular-sized horse!

Jill climbs up onto the horse's back. 'Come on,' she says to us. 'Don't just stand there. Jump on!'

Hop on board, Bobby!

We join Jill on the horse. At that moment the Story Police crash their van through the gate and drive into the paddock.

'Giddy-up!' says Jill.

At her command our tiny-horse horse gallops to the edge of the paddock and leaps over the fence!

We land on the next level down and gallop into
the Underpants Museum.

Our tiny-horse horse bumps and klunks and thumps its way through the underpants displays.

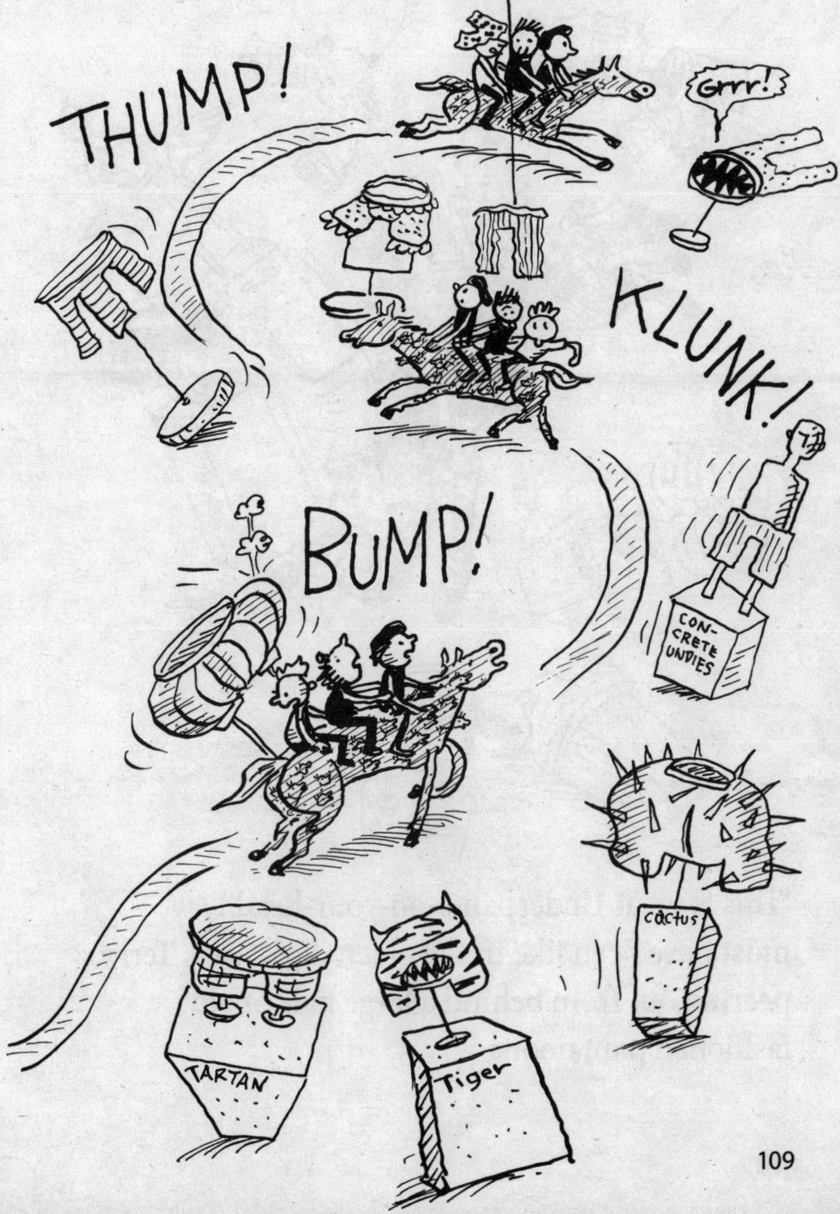
THUMP!
Grrr!
KLUNK!
BUMP!
CON-
CRETE
UNDIES
CACTUS
TARTAN
Tiger

Soon we—and our tiny-horse horse—are covered in underpants.

'This is what Underpants-on-your-head Day must have been like in the olden days!' says Terry, peering out from behind a large pair of old-fashioned pantaloons.

Our tiny-horse horse gallops through the museum, out the other side and into the big top circus tent.

Horse

We ride around the ring and the crowd cheers.
They think we're part of the show!

There's a loud honking sound behind us. I look around. We're being chased by about twenty clowns jammed into one small clown car. The audience laughs and claps.

'I wish those clowns would stop honking their horn,' says Jill. 'The tiny horses don't like it.'

Jill's right. Our tiny-horse horse is shaking and quivering with fear.

Our horse falls apart and we land on our backs in the sawdust. The tiny horses scatter in all directions.

We hear the Story Police siren.

'Oh, no!' says Terry. 'Here come the Story Police!'

The clown car screeches to a stop beside us and all the clowns pile out.

'Here,' says a clown. 'Take our car. We'll hold them off with our confetti cannon while you escape. We don't like the Story Police any more than you do—they're even worse than the Fun Police!'

'Thanks!' I say.

We jump into the car. I grab the wheel and rev the engine.

As we speed out of the tent we hear the boom of the confetti cannon and the roar of the crowd behind us.

## CHAPTER 6

# DRIVE! WAIT!

We drive out of the tent, down the branch, past the photo-bombing booth and straight into the traffic school.

I look behind me. The Story Police are hot on our trail.

'Faster, Andy!' says Jill. 'They're gaining on us!'

'Okay, hold tight!' I say. 'I may have to break a few traffic-school rules.'

I wrench the wheel and pull out into the lane of traffic coming the other way.

'Watch out for that bus full of rabbits!' shouts Terry.

I swerve back into our lane. The rabbit bus zooms past and then I swerve back out again.

'Look out!' says Jill. 'There's a duck crossing ahead—and a whole family of ducks are crossing right now!'

Quack!

'Hold on to your hats,' I say. 'We're going off-road!'

I swerve off the road and the clown car skids …

120

and plummets right off the edge of
the traffic-school level.

We fall and fall and fall until …

we crash through the roof of the waiting room and come to a stop.

'Get out of that car at once!' shouts the receptionist. 'This is a *waiting* room, not a *driving* room!'

'Sorry,' I say.

We get out of the car and run across the room towards the exit.

'STOP!' says the receptionist. 'You have to wait until your names are called.'

'But we don't have time to wait,' I explain.

'Then you shouldn't have come in here!' she says.

'We couldn't help it,' I say. 'We're being chased by the Story Police. They'll be here any minute!'

'Well they will just have to wait, too,' she says. 'No exceptions!'

Sure enough, the police arrive within moments. 'Stop right there!' says the police chief. 'You are all under arrest!'

'*Nobody* is placing *anybody* under arrest!' says the receptionist sternly.

'But these people are dangerous criminals!' says the chief.

'That may be the case,' says the receptionist, 'but this isn't an *arresting* room—it's a *waiting* room, and you have to wait until your name is called. That's the rule and I would think that you, a member of the police force, would want to set a good example.'

'Oh, all right then,' grumbles the chief. 'We'll wait.'

We wait …

and we wait …

and we wait …

and we wait.

We wait high.

We wait low.

We wait fast.

We wait slow.

We *don't* go …

and we *don't* go …

and we *don't* go ...

and we *don't* go.

'Andy, Terry and Jill?' says the receptionist.

We all jump up.

'Yes, that's us!' I say.

'You may leave,' she says. 'Thank you for waiting.'

'No!' says the police chief, jumping to his feet. 'Don't let them get away!'

'Please sit down and wait your turn,' says the receptionist. 'You know very well they were here before you.'

'But—' splutters the chief.

'No exceptions!' says the receptionist. 'You know the rule.'

We run out of the waiting room and down
a branch towards … the Door of Doom!

Terry reaches for the handle.

'No, Terry,' I say, 'don't open it!'

'Why not?' he says.

'Because it's the *Door of Doom*, that's why not!'
I say. 'You'll be doomed if you go in there!'

'But if we stay here we'll be even *more* doomed—the Story Police will catch us,' says Terry. 'Come on!'

He opens the door and runs through.

The door slams shut behind him with a resounding clang of doom.

Jill and I look at each other in shock.

'I can't believe he did that!' I say. 'I told him *never* to open the Door of Doom and now he's gone and done it!'

We hear loud footsteps and whistles. The Story Police are coming!

Jill reaches for the handle.

'What are you doing?' I say.

'Going in, of course,' she says.

'But it's the Door of DOOM!' I say.

'I know,' says Jill, 'but Terry has already gone in. I figure if we're going to be doomed, we may as well all be doomed together. Come on, let's go.'

She has a point, I guess. It *is* the Door of Doom,
but then Terry and Jill *are* my friends.

Jill opens the door and steps through.

I take a deep breath … and follow her—

## CHAPTER 7

# STORYTELLING JAIL

into a jail cell!

The Door of Doom clangs shut behind us.

'Andy! Jill!' says Terry, rushing towards us. 'I'm *so* glad you're here! I thought I was doomed to be locked up alone forever!'

'But you've only been here for a few seconds,' I say.

'Really?' says Terry. 'It felt much longer.'

'Keep quiet in there!' says a voice through the gloom on the other side of the bars.

'Who said that?' says Jill.

'I did,' says the chief of the Story Police, stepping up close to our cell. 'Thought you could get away, did you? Well, we've got you now!'

'But you can't just put people in jail for no reason!' I say.

'Oh, we've got our reasons,' says the chief, 'and plenty of them. You are hereby charged with crimes against good and proper storytelling, including the use of outlandish plots, ridiculous characters, silly names, needless repetition—

I repeat *needless repetition*—too much detail in some places, not enough in others, lack of worthy life lessons, poor eating habits, unlikely escapes, gratuitous violence, time-wasting chases and, worst of all, clichéd endings, such as *it was all just a dream* … need I go on?'

'I can explain!' I say.

'Don't explain it to *me*,' says the chief. 'Explain it to the *judge*.'

The chief opens the cell door …

marches us to a courtroom …

and puts us in the dock.

'Order in the court!' says the bailiff. 'Court now in session. Judge Pumpkin Scones presiding.'

'I object!' says Terry.

'To what?' says Judge Pumpkin Scones. 'The trial hasn't even begun.'

'That's what I object to,' says Terry. 'I don't *want* the trial to begin.'

'Well you should have thought about that before you broke so many storytelling rules in your terrible books,' says the judge. 'What do you have to say in your defence?'

'They are *not* terrible books,' says Jill.

'I'll be the judge of that,' says the judge, 'and I say they are. Case closed. I sentence you all to a BILLION years in prison! Take the prisoners away!'

Judge Pumpkin Scones bangs her gavel. 'Court dismissed.'

We are marched back to our prison cell.

The chief pushes us inside, locks the door and throws the key out the window. 'See you in a billion years,' he says, laughing as he walks away.

'How much is a billion years?' I say. 'It seems like a long time.'

'It's a *very* long time,' says Terry. 'It's a million million years.'

'Actually,' says Jill, 'I think you'll find that a billion is a *thousand* million, not a *million* million.'

'Oh, well, that doesn't seem so bad then,' I say. 'I don't know much about maths, but I do know that a *thousand* is a *lot* less than a million!'

'Yes, but we're talking about YEARS!' says Terry. 'It's still a THOUSAND MILLION YEARS and a THOUSAND MILLION YEARS is a long, long time. I'VE GOTTA GET OUT OF HERE, I'M GOING CRAZY! I CAN'T STAND BEING LOCKED UP LIKE THIS!'

'Calm down,' I say. 'We have to think our way out of this—not panic.'

'Maybe we could tunnel our way out?' says Jill.

'Well, we could,' says Terry, 'but we don't have anything to dig with.'

'What about your spooncil, Terry?' says Jill. 'Do you have it with you?'

'Yes,' says Terry. 'It's up my nose, where I always keep it, but it's pretty high up. I need to sneeze to get it out. Has anybody got any pepper?'

I look around. 'Yes,' I say. 'There's a pile of pepper over here.'

I grab a handful and blow it into Terry's face.

Terry throws his head back. 'Ah … ah … ah … ACHOO!'

The spooncil flies out of Terry's left nostril and into his hand. He immediately drops to his knees and begins scraping at the stone floor with the spoon end of the spooncil.

He scrapes ... and scrapes ... and scrapes ...

and scrapes ... and scrapes ... and scrapes ...

and scrapes ... and scrapes ... and scrapes ...

and scrapes ... and scrapes ... and scrapes ...

and scrapes ... and scrapes ... and scrapes ...

and scrapes ... and scrapes ... and scrapes ...

153

and scrapes ... and scrapes ... and scrapes ...

and scrapes ... and scrapes ... and scrapes ...

and scrapes ... and scrapes ... and scrapes ...

and scrapes ... and scrapes ... and scrapes ...

'How's the tunnel going?' I say. 'Is it finished yet?'

'Not quite,' says Terry. 'But it's deep enough to get a little bit of my finger in. See?'

'That's good,' I say. 'Keep going!'

He scrapes …    and scrapes …    and scrapes …

and scrapes …    and scrapes …    and scrapes …

and scrapes ... and scrapes ... and scrapes ...

and scrapes ... and scrapes ... and scrapes ...

and scrapes ... and scrapes ... and scrapes ...

and scrapes ... and scrapes ... and scrapes ...

and scrapes ...     and scrapes ...     and scrapes ...

and scrapes ...     and scrapes ...     and scrapes ...

and scrapes ...     and scrapes ...     and scrapes ...

and scrapes ...     and scrapes ...     and scrapes ...

'Are you finished yet?' I say.

'Not quite,' says Terry. 'But the hole's getting deeper. I can get almost *half* my finger in now!'

'Great scraping, Terry!' says Jill. 'Keep going!'

He scrapes ...     and scrapes ...     and scrapes ...

and scrapes ...     and scrapes ...     and scrapes ...

and scrapes ...     and scrapes ...     and scrapes ...

and scrapes ...     and scrapes ...     and scrapes ...

and scrapes ...     and scrapes ...     and scrapes ...

and scrapes ...     and scrapes ...     and scrapes ...

and scrapes … and scrapes … and scrapes …

and scrapes … and scrapes … and scrapes …

and scrapes … and scrapes … and scrapes …

and scrapes … and scrapes … and scrapes …

and scrapes …   and scrapes …   and scrapes …

and scrapes …   and scrapes …   and scrapes …

and scrapes …   and scrapes …   and scrapes …

and scrapes …   and scrapes …   and scrapes …

'Are you finished yet?' says Jill.

'Not quite,' says Terry, 'but I can practically get my *whole* finger in now.'

'It's no use!' I yell. 'This is going to take at least a *billion* years … possibly even a *billion* billion, and we've only got a thousand million! I'VE GOTTA GET OUT OF HERE, I'M GOING CRAZY! I CAN'T STAND BEING LOCKED UP LIKE THIS!'

Terry studies his spooncil. 'I think I've got a better idea,' he says. 'We could use a dot.'

'Oh no,' I say. 'Not *more* dots! That's what started all this trouble in the first place.'

'Let's at least *hear* his idea,' says Jill. 'I don't want to be stuck in here any more than you two do. I'VE GOTTA GET OUT OF HERE, I'M GOING CRAZY! I CAN'T STAND BEING LOCKED UP LIKE THIS!'

'It's okay, Jill,' says Terry. He turns his spooncil around and uses the pencil to draw a really big dot on the ground.

'How is that going to help?' I say.

'It's an escape hatch,' says Terry, drawing a handle on top of the dot. He pulls the handle up to reveal a hole with a ladder going down into the darkness.

Say 'Hi' to Silky from us, Jill.

'But where does it go?' I say.

'Away from here,' says Terry, already standing on the ladder, 'and that's all I care about.'

'Me too,' says Jill, climbing down after him.

I shrug and follow them, closing the hatch behind me.

We climb down the ladder and come to a tunnel.
Then we get down on our hands and knees and
start crawling.

## CHAPTER 8

# THE TALE OF LITTLE PETER POOPYPANTS

We crawl and we crawl and we crawl and we crawl.

We crawl fast.

We crawl slow.

We crawl high.

We crawl low.

We go and we go and we go and we go … until we see a glimmer of light.

'At last!' I say. 'Freedom!'

We climb out of the tunnel into the middle of a large vegetable patch.

A little rabbit dressed in a blue jacket and a pair of brown pants hops towards us. 'Quick!' he says. 'Follow me or Farmer McRabbit-Grabber will get you!'

'Who's Farmer McRabbit-Grabber?' says Terry.
   The little rabbit points to an angry, red-faced farmer running towards us. 'He is!'

'Just wait until I get my rabbit-grabbing hands on you, Little Peter Poopypants!' booms the farmer. 'Then you'll be sorry!'

We run after the little rabbit as fast as we can.

'Quick, hide in here!' says the rabbit, hopping into a large barrel.

We dive in after him.

'Shhhh!' he says, putting a paw to his lips. 'Don't make a sound.'

We hear the angry farmer go stomping past.

The rabbit pokes his head up out of the barrel. 'He's gone,' he says, 'but we should stay in here a little longer … just in case.'

'Why is he so angry at you?' whispers Jill. 'How could anybody be mad at such an adorable little rabbit?'

'I guess you haven't read the book,' says the rabbit.

'What book?' says Jill.

'This one.' He takes a book out of his jacket pocket and hands it to Jill.

This one →

The Tale of
Little Peter
Poopypants

story and pictures by
Beatrix Potty

Jill laughs. 'Oh, I've read that book!' she says. 'So you're *that* Little Peter Poopypants. No wonder Farmer McRabbit-Grabber is angry with you.'

'Why, what happened?' I say.

'How about I read the book to you?' says Jill. 'It's pretty funny and it will explain everything.'

'Oh, goody, I love funny stories that explain everything,' says Terry.

ONCE upon a time there were four little rabbits, and their names were Hoppy, Poppy, Lippety-Loppity and Little Peter Poopypants.

old cabbage

They lived with their mother in a cosy three-bedroom rabbit hole with views of tree roots from every window.

'NOW, my dears,' said Mother one morning, 'I must go out. While I'm gone you may go down to the river and gather blackberries but, whatever you do, do not go into Farmer McRabbit-Grabber's garden or he will grab you and give you to Mrs McRabbit-Grabber to cook into a pie, just like your poor father, Big Pop Poopypants.'

HOPPY, Poppy and Lippety-Loppity, who were good little bunnies, went down to the river to gather blackberries.

BUT Little Peter Poopypants, who was very naughty, as well as very poopy, ran straight away to Farmer McRabbit-Grabber's garden and squeezed himself and his little poopy pants under the gate!

FIRST he visited the potatoes and he had a little nibble and he did a little poop.

Next he visited the peas and he had a little nibble and he did a little poop.

AND then he visited the pumpkins in Farmer McRabbit-Grabber's precious pumpkin patch and he … well, I think you can guess what he did.

THEN Little Peter Poopypants began to feel rather tired from all that nibbling and pooping, so he lay down in the parsley for a short rest— but he soon fell fast asleep.

WHILE Peter was sleeping, Farmer McRabbit-Grabber came along and found him.

'Aha! You'll be sorry you ever pooped up my garden,' he said as he grabbed Little Peter Poopypants roughly and dropped him into his sack. 'I'll take you home tonight to Mrs McRabbit-Grabber and she will bake you into a delicious rabbit pie!'

FARMER McRabbit-Grabber tied up the top of the sack and went back to his work. By and by Little Peter Poopypants woke up, realised what had happened and started to cry. 'Oh no, I'm trapped in Farmer McRabbit-Grabber's sack—how will I ever get out?'

JUST then, along came a mouse called Thomasina Tittle-Tattle. She heard Little Peter Poopypants crying. 'Don't worry, Little Peter, Poopypants,' said Thomasina Tittle-Tattle. 'With my sharp little teeth I shall gnaw a hole in the sack and you will soon be able to escape!'

THOMASINA Tittle-Tattle worked quickly and soon there was a tiny hole in the bottom of the sack.

CHOMP! CHOMP! CHOMP!

Little Peter Poopypants thanked Thomasina Tittle-Tattle and wriggled through the hole, but not before filling the sack with enough poop to trick Farmer McRabbit-Grabber into thinking he was still in there.

WHEN Farmer McRabbit-Grabber had finished his work he came back, picked up the sack and carried it home to Mrs McRabbit-Grabber and asked her to cook the contents of the sack into a pie.

RAFF
RAFF
RAFF

LATER that day, when Mrs McRabbit-Grabber opened the sack and saw what was in it, she thought it was odd that her husband wanted it cooked for his dinner but, nevertheless, she did exactly as he had asked.

stink cloud

COME dinner time, Farmer McRabbit-Grabber sat down to eat his pie. He took a big mouthful and then spat it all out again. 'This pie is filled with poop, not rabbit!' he shouted. 'Little Peter Poopypants has tricked me! Just wait until I get my rabbit-grabbing hands on him!'

THE END

'And that's why Farmer McRabbit-Grabber hates me!' says Little Peter Poopypants. 'Because I'm cleverer and smarterer than he is.'

'And because you made him eat a great big poopy pie!' shouts Terry, laughing.

See-through barrel picture

'Quiet, Terry,' I say. 'Farmer McRabbit-Grabber might hear you and then he'll bake us *all* into a pie!'

'Too late!' says Jill. 'I think he's already heard us. Here he comes!'

We hear heavy footsteps stomping towards the barrel.

'Aha!' says Farmer McRabbit-Grabber, peering down at us. 'Four little rabbits for my dinner!'

He picks up the barrel and tips us into his sack.

'No, you're making a big mistake!' says Terry, as we tumble in. 'We're not rabbits!'

'What's this?' says Farmer McRabbit-Grabber. '*Not* rabbits?' He peers into the sack. 'I know who you are. You're worse than rabbits—you're criminals! I saw your WANTED poster in the post office this morning.'

WANTED
DEAD OR ALIVE

ANDY    TERRY    JILL

FOR CRIMES AGAINST STORYTELLING
117 MILLION BILLION DOLLAR REWARD!
If found, please contact the Story Police

'This must be my lucky day!' says Farmer McRabbit-Grabber. 'A one hundred and seventeen million billion dollar reward *and* rabbit pie for dinner! I'll go and notify the Story Police right now. And, in the meantime, I'll hang the sack up on this hook to make sure none of you escape.'

Farmer McRabbit-Grabber ties the end of the sack shut and we feel ourselves being lifted high up into the air.

'Oh no!' I say. 'It's just like in Little Peter Poopypants' story!'

'Why don't we call Thomasina Tittle-Tattle and ask her to gnaw a hole in the sack for us?' says Jill.

'It's no use calling Thomasina Tittle-Tattle,' says
Little Peter Poopypants. 'She was eaten by Katy
Kitten-Whiskers just last week.'

'Oh, that's very sad,' says Jill.

'Not for Katy Kitten-Whiskers, it wasn't,' says
Peter. 'She said Thomasina Tittle-Tattle was
delicious!'

'We don't need Thomasina Tittle-Tattle,' says
Terry. 'I can draw a dot that will make a perfect
hole for us to escape through.'

Terry uses the pencil end of his spooncil to draw a dot at the bottom of the sack.

Jill, Little Peter Poopypants and I all squeeze through it and lower ourselves to the ground. Terry comes last, peeling the dot off the bottom of the sack as he exits.

'Farmer McRabbit-Grabber will never figure out how we got out of there,' says Little Peter Poopypants.

'But what if he reads our book?' I say.

'We haven't even *written* our book yet,' says Terry. 'And by the time we do, we'll be safely back in the treehouse. Look, I've drawn another dot—and this one can fly! Jump on, everybody.'

'Wow, this is just like a magic flying carpet,' says Jill, 'except it's a magic flying DOT!'

'Can you drop me off at my burrow?' says Little
Peter Poopypants. 'It's just down there near that
big tree.'

We fly down and hover while Little Peter
Poopypants hops off the dot.

'Thanks for the ride,' he says. 'And thanks for
helping me escape from Farmer McRabbit-Grabber!'

'It was our pleasure,' I say. 'And when we get home I'll send you a pair of emergency anti-pooping pull-ups from our Underpants Museum. Then you will be able to visit Farmer McRabbit-Grabber's garden any time you want and he'll never know you've been there!'

'Yay!' says Little Peter Poopypants.

We wave goodbye to Little Peter Poopypants and our dot rises into the sky and flies up, up and away.

## CHAPTER 9

# THE SPLAT IN THE HAT

We fly

And we fly

And we fly

And we fly.

We fly fast.

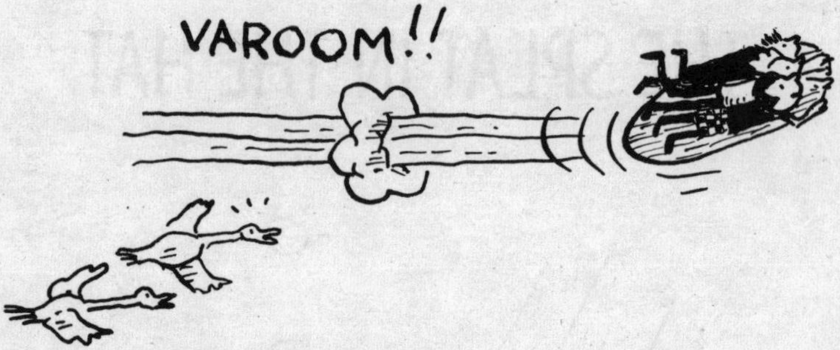
VAROOM!!

We fly slow.

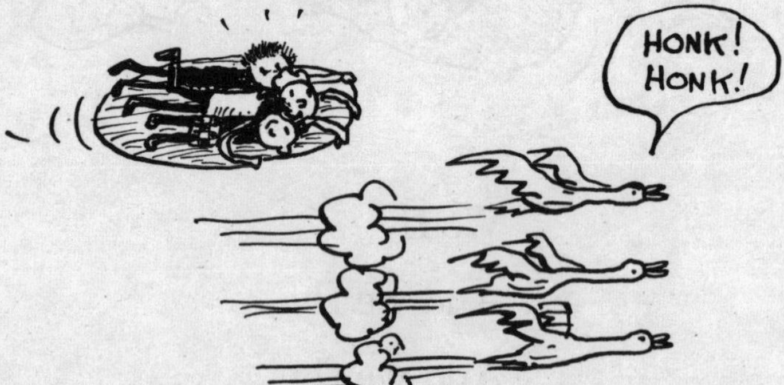
HONK!
HONK!

We fly high.

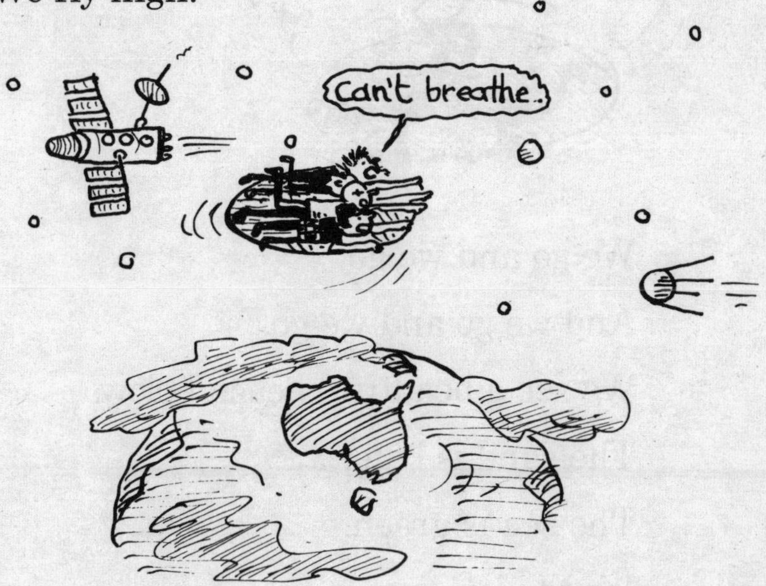
Can't breathe...

We fly low.

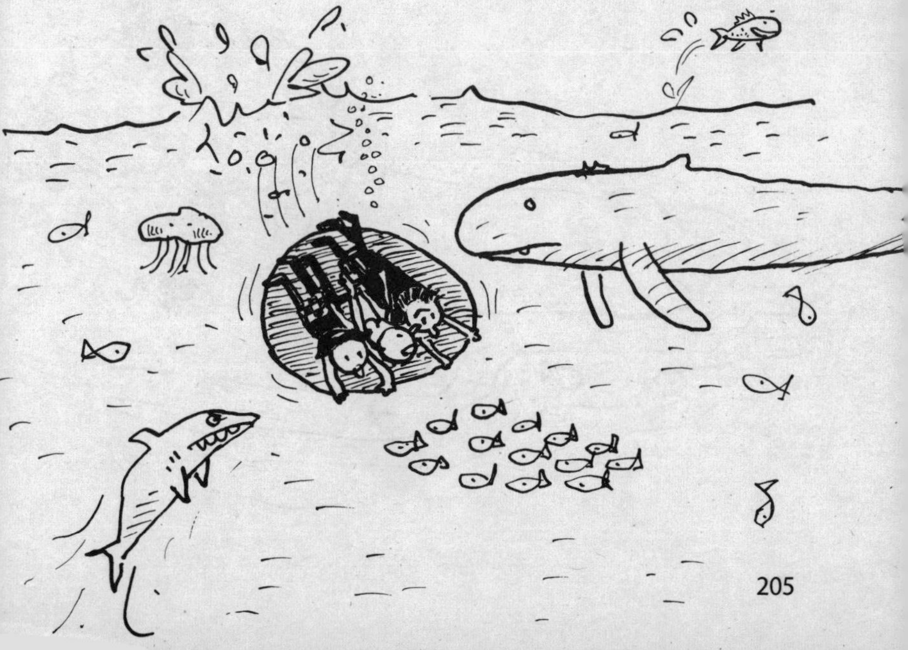

Flying
Dot

We go and we go

And we go and we go.

We see a beautiful beach below.

The sand is blue,

The sea is green.

It's the loveliest beach

We've ever seen!

We land the dot
Beneath a tree
Where we find a rug
With food for three
And a sign that says
*This picnic's free!*

We sit on the rug
And start to eat—
But then a big fat SPLAT
Makes us jump to our feet!

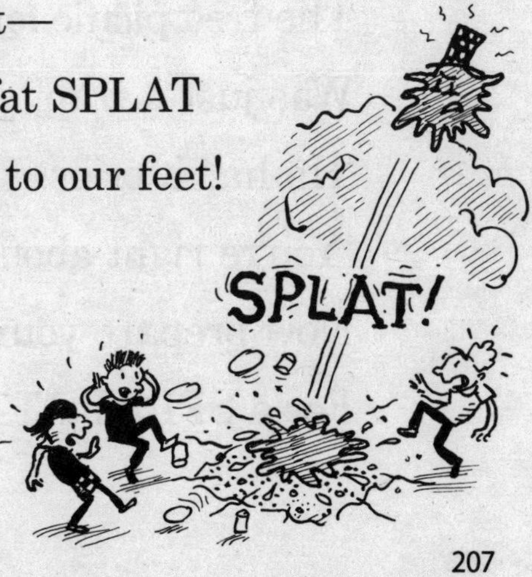
SPLAT!

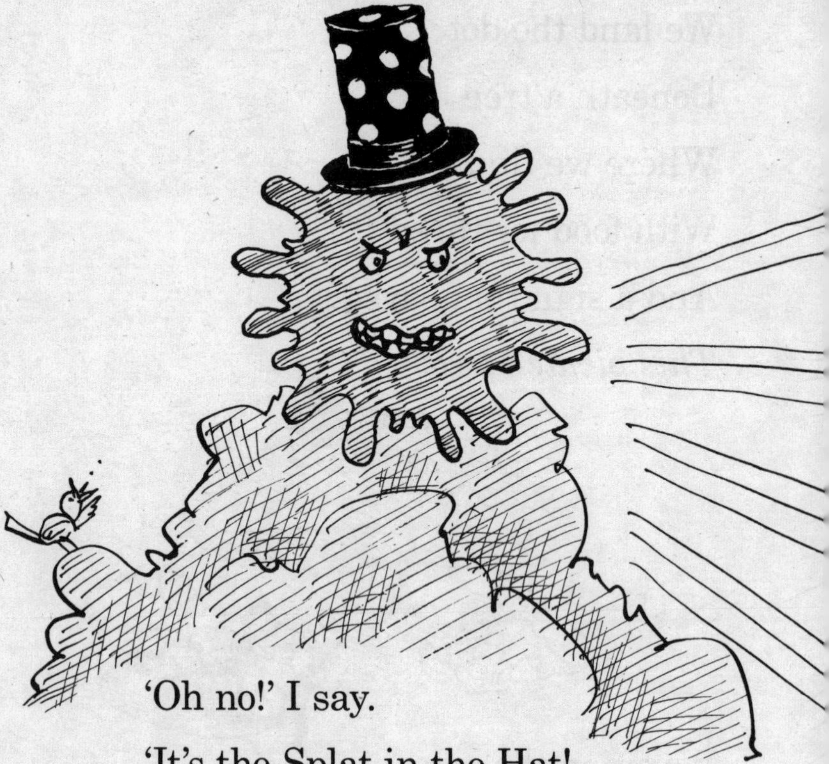

'Oh no!' I say.
'It's the Splat in the Hat!
The free picnic for three
Was just a trap!'
'Ha-ha,' it cries.
'You're right about that!
Now prepare yourselves
For a SPLAT ATTACK!'

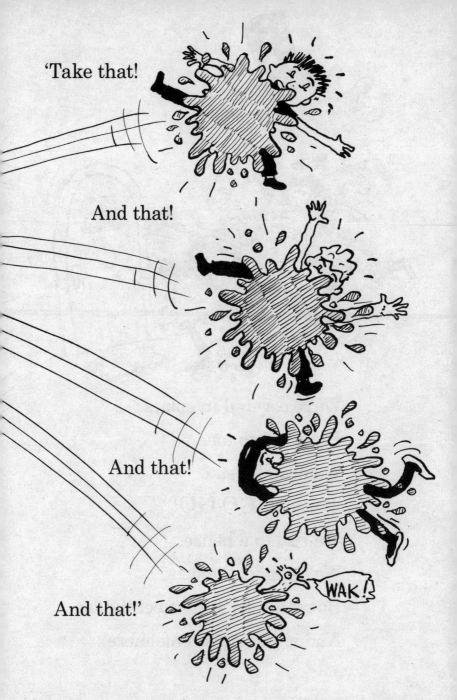

'Take that!

And that!

And that!

And that!'

We're covered in splats

From top to toe.

'Come on!' I say.

'Let's GO GO GO!'

We run to a house.

We bang on the door.

But the splat's right behind us

And it splats us some more!

The door opens wide
And two children say
'Quick, hide in here
Till the splat goes away.'
'Thanks!' we say
As we run on through.
But the splat is too fast—
And it gets in too!

It splats the wall!

It splats the floor!

It splats the window!

And it splats the door!

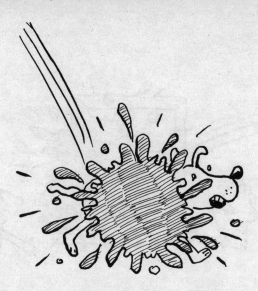

It splats the dog!

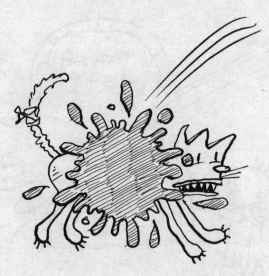

It splats the cat!

It splats the fish!

And it splats the mat!

'Oh, no!' cry the children.

'Boo hoo, boo hoo!

Our house is all splattered

And we are too.'

'Don't cry,' says Terry.

'I know what to do.

Prepare to meet

Dot One and Dot Two!'

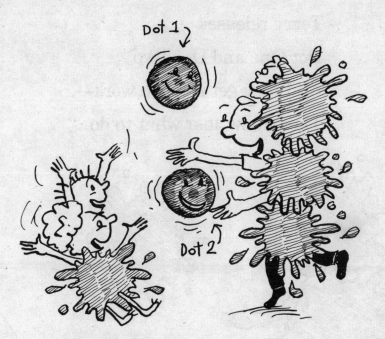

'These amazing dots
Will make your home neat
Because splats are their
Favourite things to eat!
These de-splatting dots
Eat splats for lunch
And breakfast and dinner
And snacks and brunch!'

Terry releases
Dot One and Dot Two
And they get right to work—
They know JUST what to do.

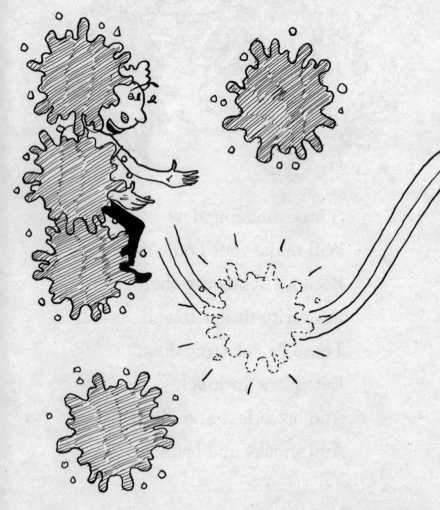

They bite and they munch!

They chomp and they crunch!

They gobble and guzzle and slurp!

(And every so often

They stop all their chewing

And let out a very large burp.)

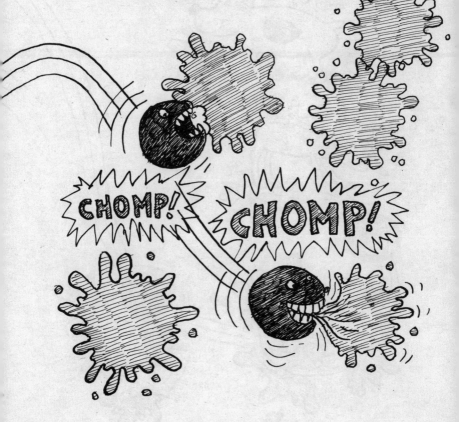

They de-splat the dog!
They de-splat the cat!
They de-splat the fish!
And they de-splat the mat!

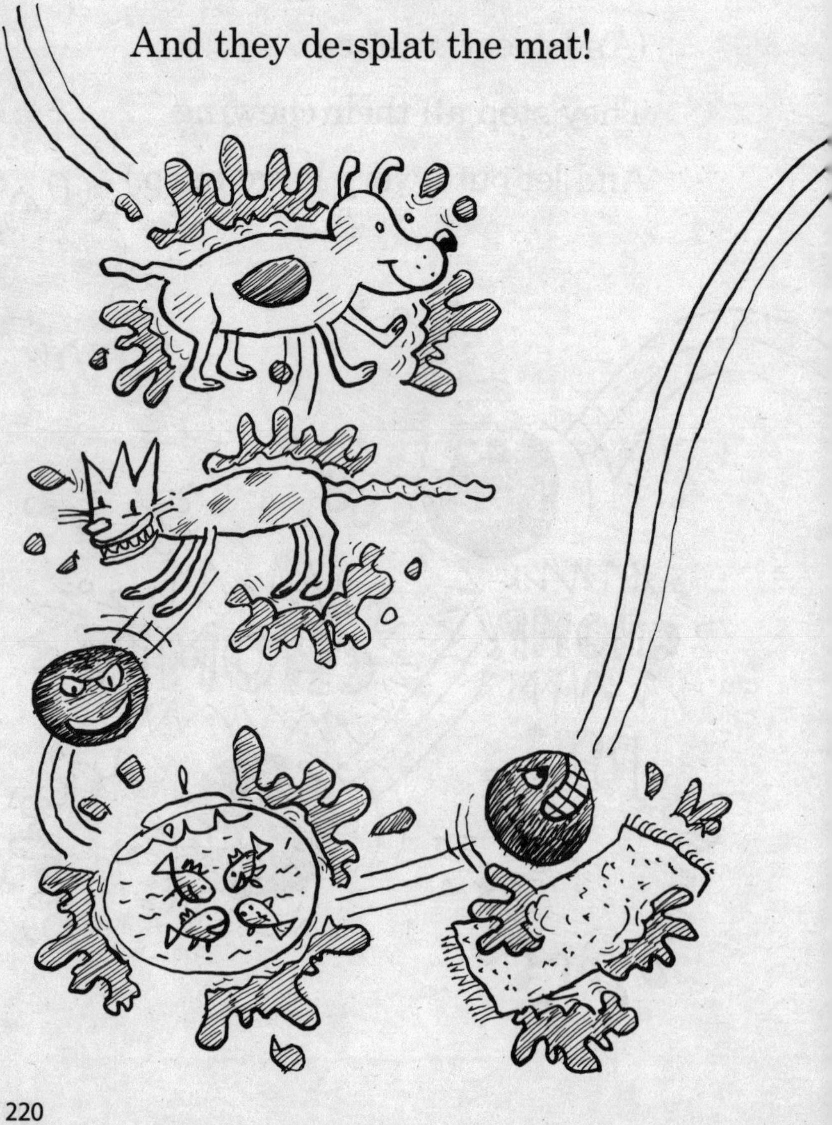

They de-splat the wall!
They de-splat the floor!
They de-splat the window!
And they de-splat the door!

They de-splat Terry
And Jill and me
And in no time at all
We're completely splat free!

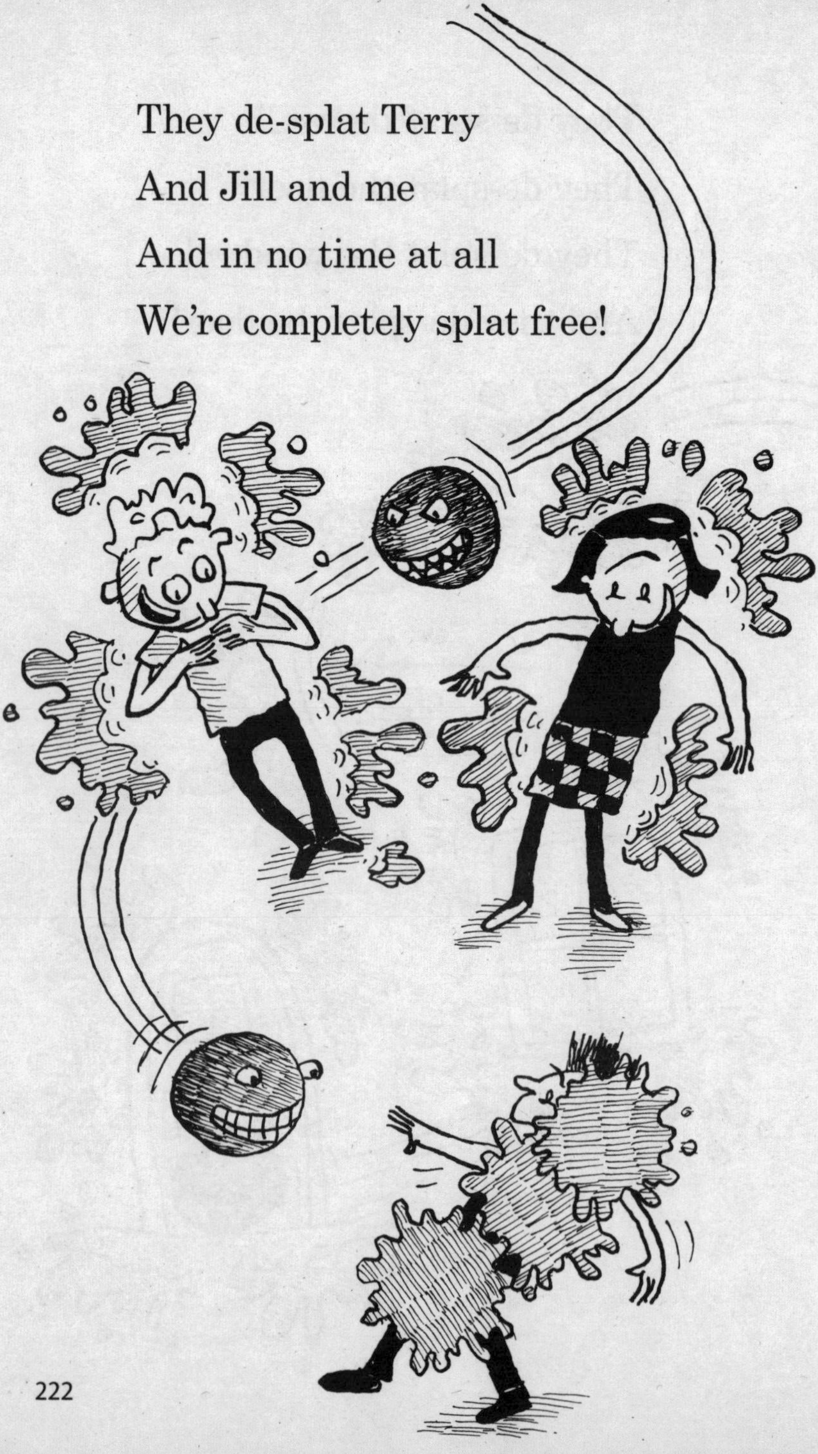

They de-splat the girl

And they de-splat the boy.

And they are so happy

They shout with joy:

'Hooray! Hoorah!

Callooh! Callay!

Dot One and Dot Two

Have saved the day!'

'They came to our rescue

When it really mattered

And now everything's clean

And completely de-splattered!'

'My splats! My splats!'
Cries the Splat in the Hat.
'Oh why, why, why
Did you have to do that?'
The Splat in the Hat
Begins to cry.
A big fat tear
Rolls out of each eye.

It cries.

And cries.

And cries.

And cries.

In fact, it cries so much,
That I'm happy to say
It completely washes
Itself away!

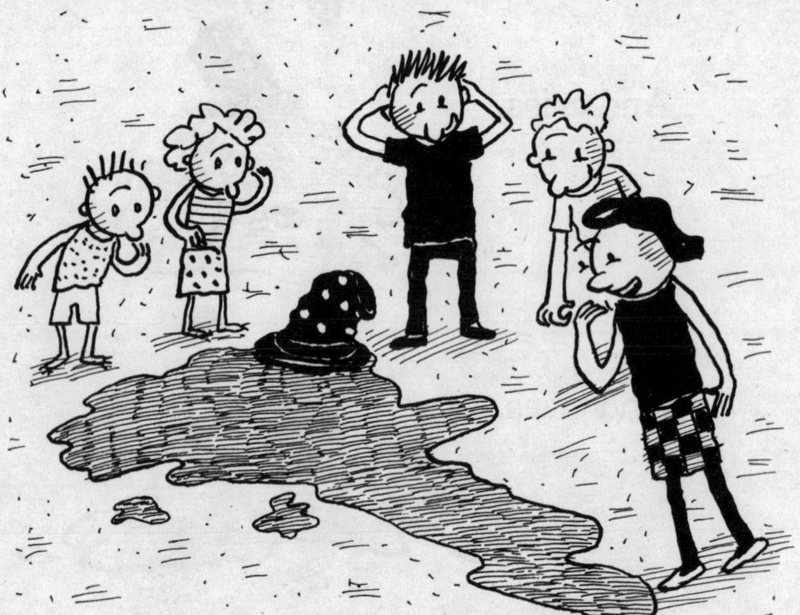

And that is the end
Of the big bad splat—
And all that is left
Is its dotty old hat.

'Good work, Terry.

Well done,' says Jill.

'But I must confess

That I'm feeling quite ill.

For the Story Police

Are drawing near.

And being captured

Is what I fear.'

'Don't worry,' says Terry.

'Fear not! Fear not!

For I have got

Another dot—

The sort of dot

That can become a ...

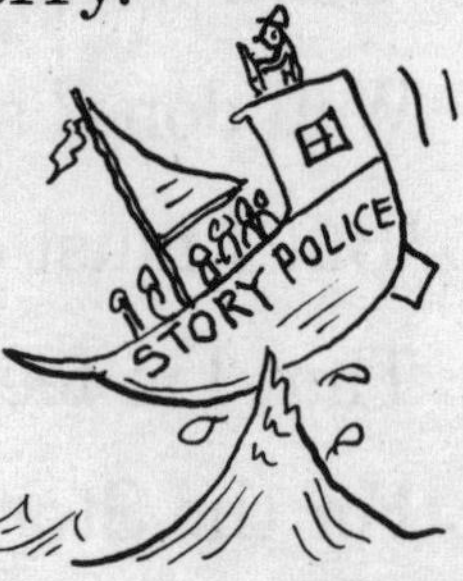
STORY POLICE

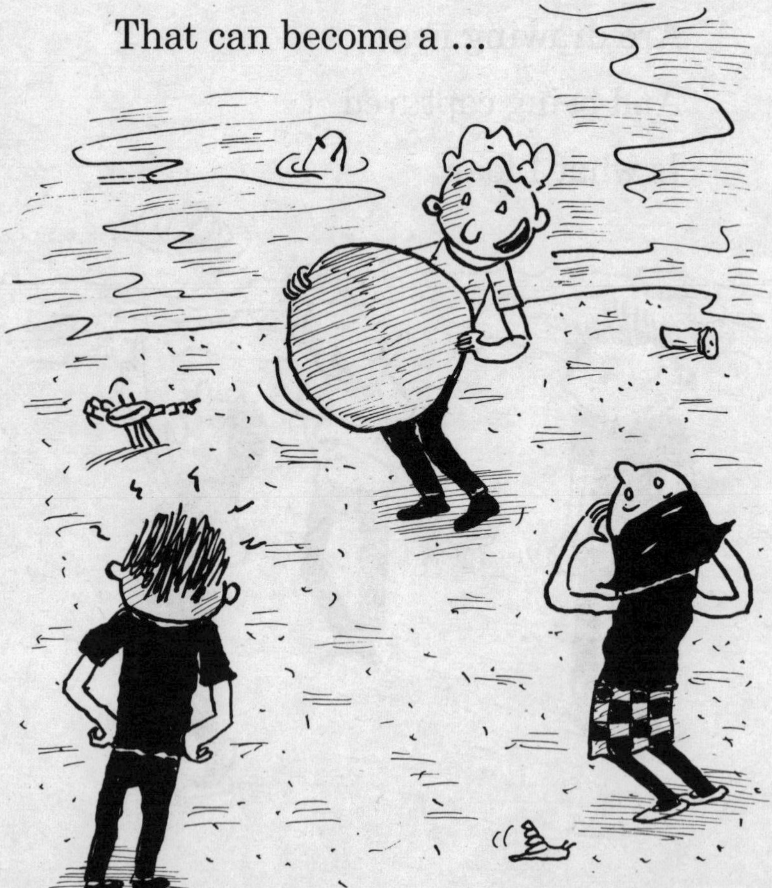

# yacht!'

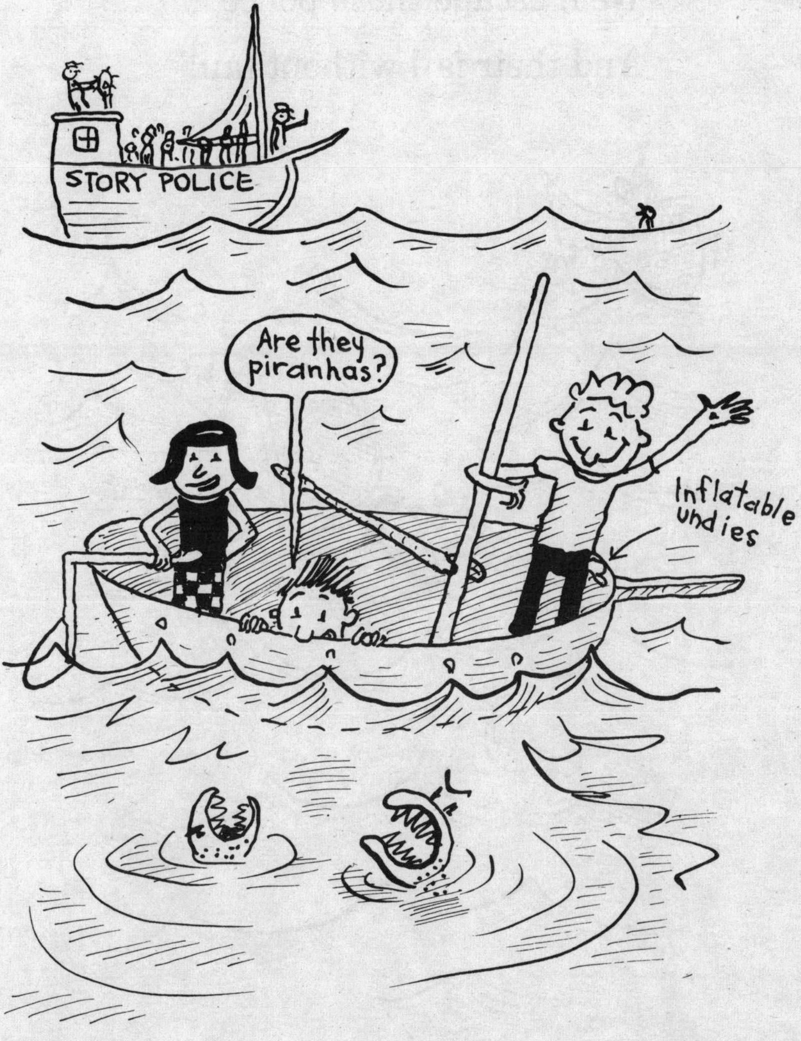
STORY POLICE
Are they piranhas?
Inflatable undies

'And my inflatable underpants
Will make a great sail.
We'll escape those police
And their jail without fail!'

# CHAPTER 10

# WHERE THE FILED THINGS ARE

We sail and we sail and we sail and we sail.

We sail fast.

We sail slow.

We sail high.

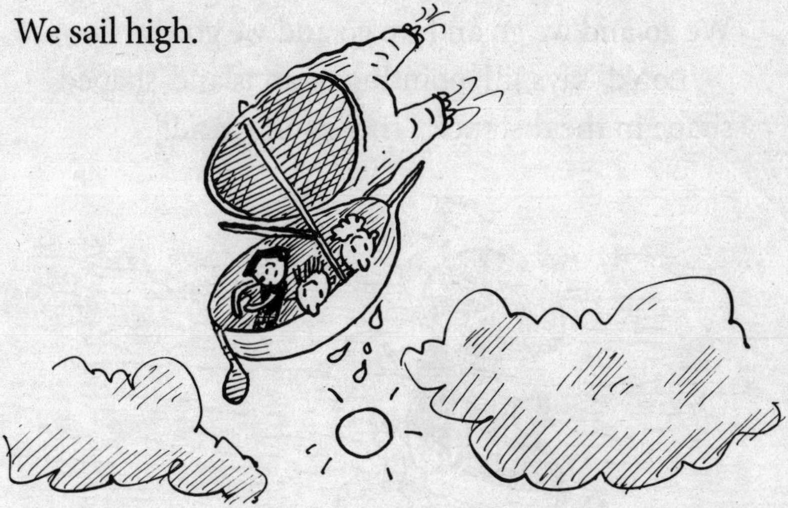

We sail low.

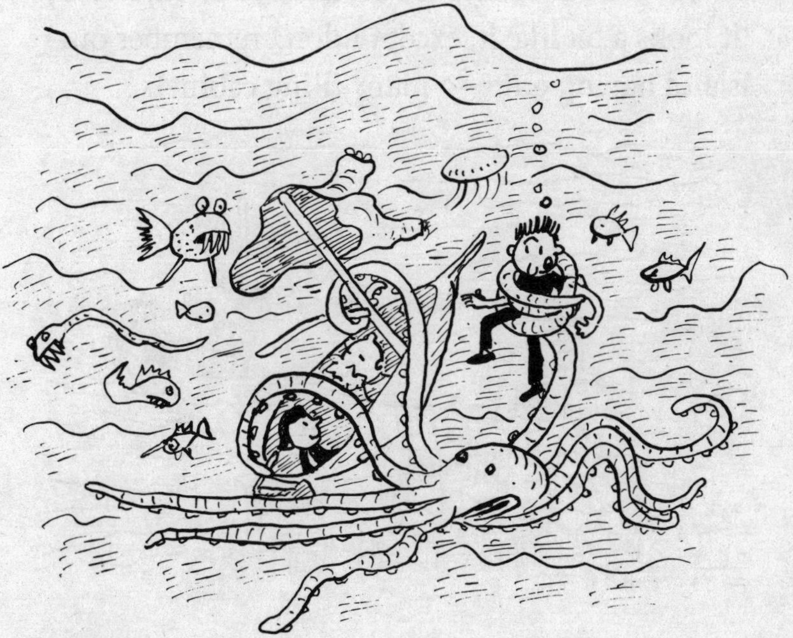

We go and we go and we go and we go.

'Look!' says Jill, pointing to an island-shaped shape in the distance. 'There's an island!'

'I hope it's our treehouse desert island!' says Terry. 'It looks a bit like it, except I don't remember our island having quite so many filing cabinets.'

'Our island doesn't have *any* filing cabinets,'
I say. 'And this one has *stacks* of them. Stacks
and stacks, all stacked on top of each other!'

THE DAY WE SAILED TO AN ISLAND THAT HAD STACKS AND STACKS OF FILING CABINETS ALL STACKED ON TOP OF EACH OTHER.

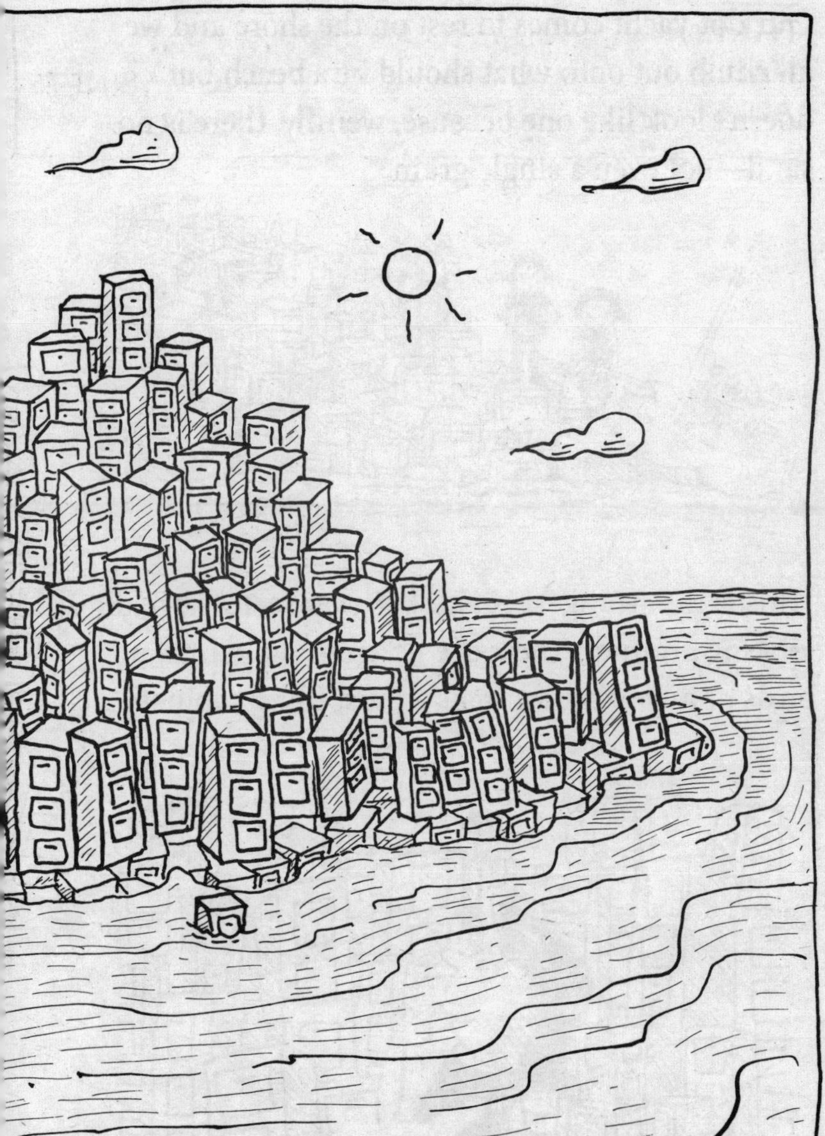

Our dot-yacht comes to rest on the shore and we all climb out onto what should be a beach but doesn't look like one because, weirdly, there is no sand—not even a single grain.

'This is the strangest island I've ever seen,' says Jill, looking around. 'There are no trees, no plants, no birds or any other animals ... just filing cabinets.'

'I wonder what's in them?' says Terry.

'Let's have a look!' I say.

I grab the handle of a drawer marked P and try to pull it open. But it won't budge. 'It's locked,' I say.

'I think they all are,' says Terry, running from cabinet to cabinet, pulling at the drawers.

'Quiet!' says Jill. 'I can hear something. I think it's coming from that drawer you tried to open, Andy.'

We all lean in close.

'Let me out of here!' says a small voice. 'For Pete's sake, let me out of here!'

'We can't,' I shout as loudly as I can to whoever—or whatever—is in there. 'The drawer is locked!'

'Then, for Pete's sake, get a key!' says the voice. 'Try one of the drawers marked K.'

'There's one over there!' says Jill.

Terry and I run over to the cabinet and try to open the drawer, but we can't.

'This drawer is locked too,' I say.

'It doesn't matter,' says Terry. 'I can use a dot to get the keys out.'

Terry draws a large dot in the middle of the filing cabinet drawer.

He puts his hand into the dot-hole and pulls out three keys.

'One each,' he says, handing them out.

'Let's try them,' says Jill.

We rush over and open the P drawer. A blue-and-yellow parrot with a black eyepatch and a wooden leg flies out and lands in front of us.

'Thanks, me hearties,' he says. 'I thought I was going to be filed away for the rest of me days!'

'Are you a pirate?' says Terry.

'Aye, that I be!' he says. 'One-eyed Pete the pirate parakeet at your service. And who might you be?'

'I be Terry,' says Terry. 'And that be Jill and that be Andy.'

'Are you pirates too?' says One-eyed Pete.

'No,' says Terry, 'but we did all work on a pirate ship for a while.'

'Who locked you in that filing cabinet?' says Jill.

'It was that blasted filing monster,' says One-eyed Pete. 'Blast and curse its blasted filing fingers!'

'A filing monster?' says Terry. 'Hmm … that sounds a bit like the monster in Mr Big Nose's favourite book, *Where the Filed Things Are!*'

'It's a *monster* all right,' says One-eyed Pete.
'This used to be a beautiful tropical island. There
were all sorts of animals living here—turtles,
monkeys, hippos, dinosaurs, giant rabbits, seals
… until that crazy filing monster came along and
filed *everything*!'

'Do you mean there are other living creatures
trapped in these filing cabinets?' says Jill.

'Aye, Missy,' says One-eyed Pete. 'All the
drawers are stuffed full, and not only with all the
island's creatures but the rocks and trees and sand
and rivers as well!'

'But why?' says Jill. 'Why would the filing monster *do* such a thing?'

'Because it's a *filing* monster,' says One-eyed Pete. 'That's what it does.'

'Well it's not right,' says Jill. 'Let's put the island back the way it's *supposed* to be.'

THE DAY WE OPENED ALL OF THE FILING MONSTER'S FILING CABINETS AND LET THE ISLAND OUT.

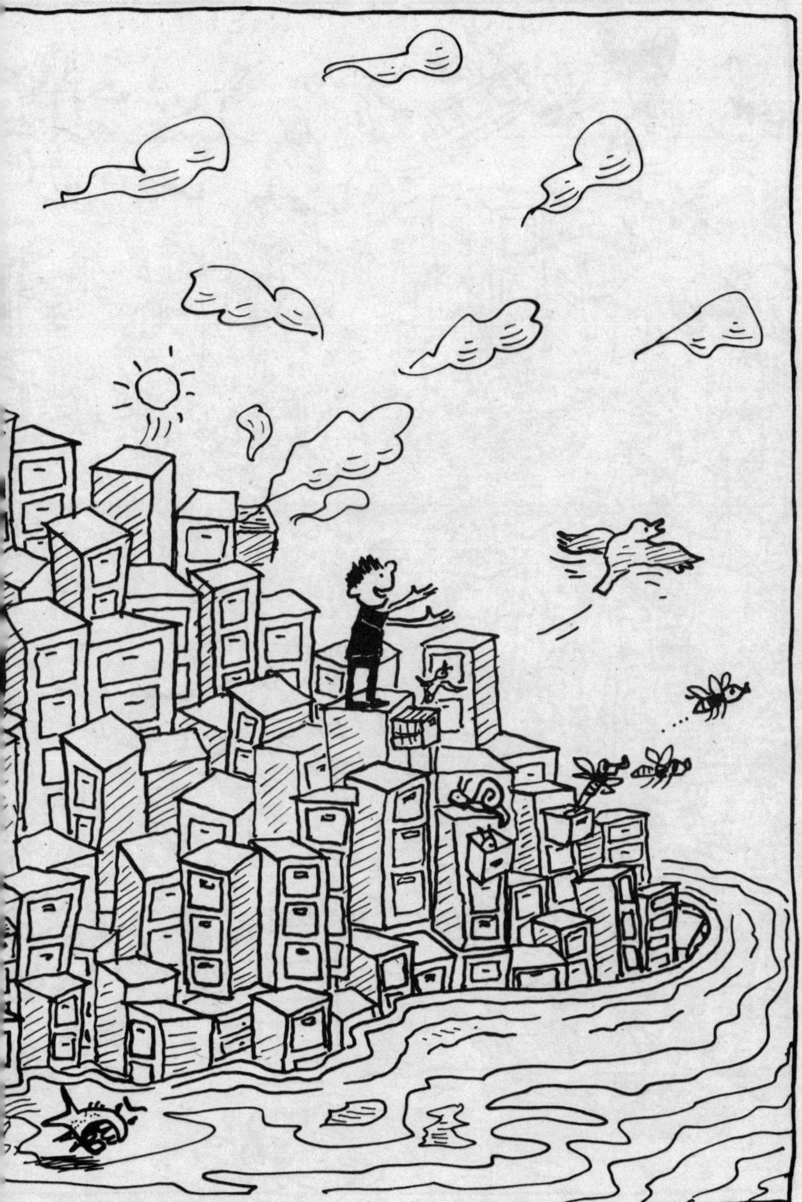

Hee, haw!

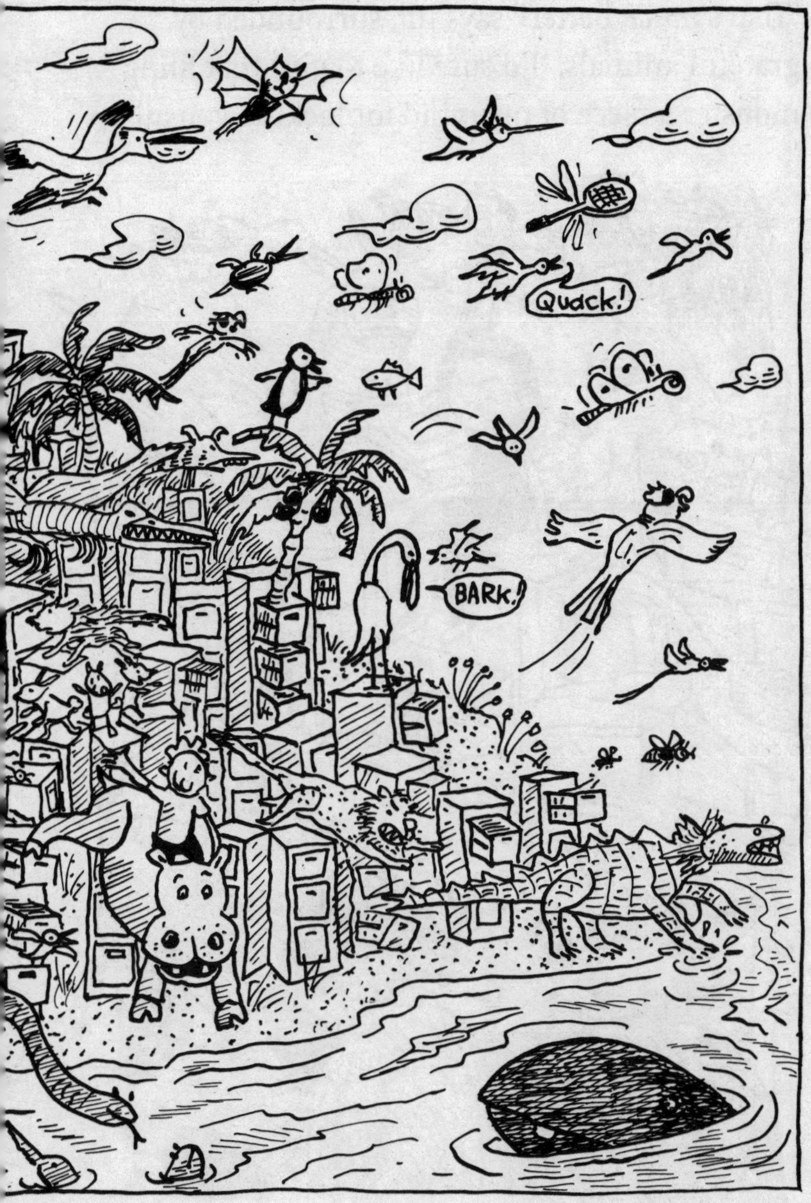
QUACK!
BARK!

'That's *much* better!' says Jill, surrounded by grateful animals. 'I'd sure like to give that filing monster a piece of my mind for locking you all up.'

'I think you might get your chance to do just that very soon,' says One-eyed Pete, as the ground begins to shake, 'because HERE IT COMES!'

**THUD!**

**THUD!**

**THUD!**

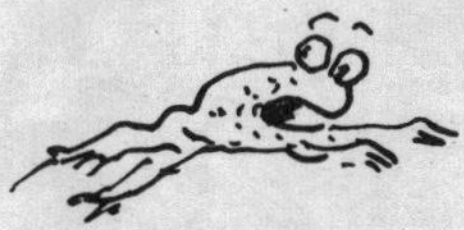

We can hear the monster chanting as it gets closer to us.

'FEE FILE FO FUM!
I LOVE FILING-IT IS FUN!
FEE FUM FO FILE!
IT'S FUN TO FILE ON MY FILING ISLE!'

'I'm outta here!' says Pete. 'When the filing monster finds out what's happened it's going to be MAD!'

And with that, Pete flies off towards the shore, lands on our dot-yacht and sails away.

The rest of the animals fly and run and scurry and scuttle and dive for cover.

COW

I look around.

I'm the only one left.

Everybody's gone. Even Jill and Terry are nowhere to be seen.

'Pssst!' says Jill, peering out of a filing cabinet drawer marked H. 'We're over here.'

'Under H for *hiding*!' says Terry.

I run and join them … just in time.

## CHAPTER 11

# Where the Filed Things Were

The monster stomps through the forest of filing cabinets and its feet sink deep into the sand, which is now back all over the ground.

'WHAT IS THIS SAND DOING HERE?' growls the monster. 'IT SHOULD BE FILED UNDER S!'

It angrily scoops up a handful of sand and marches across to a filing cabinet drawer marked S. It stares at the open drawer and roars.

'FEE FILE FO FORE!
WHO HAS OPENED UP THIS DRAWER?
FEE FILE FO FABINETS!
WHO'S BEEN MESSING WITH MY CABINETS?!'

The monster rips a coconut palm from the ground and shoves it into a drawer marked C.

It grabs an armful of rocks and drops them in a drawer marked R.

It snatches a bird from the sky and is about to shove it into a drawer marked B when Jill jumps up and yells, 'STOP! That's no way to treat birds! Birds belong in the sky where they can be free— not locked away in a drawer marked B!'

'Uh-oh,' I whisper to Terry. 'She's done it now.'

'Who are you?' says the monster.

'I'm Jill,' says Jill defiantly.

The monster glares at her.

'Did you open up all my filing cabinets?'

'Yes, I did!' says Jill. 'You had animals filed in there and it's *not right*.'

'Yes it *is*,' says the monster. 'It was *exactly* right.
I'm very good at filing. I had the snakes under S.
I had the toucans under T. And I had the lambs
under L. And I'm going to put you under M for
MEDDLING HUMANS WHO SHOULD MIND
THEIR OWN BUSINESS!'

'Animals *are* my business,' says Jill. 'I run an intergalactic animal rescue service, you know … and that *includes* animals on Earth who are trapped in filing cabinet drawers.'

'And I run a filing business,' says the monster. 'I love to file and I found an island that needed filing and that's exactly what I did until you came and messed it all up. But I'll soon fix that!'

The monster pulls the drawer all the way open and sees Terry and me.

'Aha!' it says, scooping us all up. '*More* meddling humans!'

'Put us down right now!' says Jill.

'Please!' says Terry.

'Pretty please!' I say.

'I'll put you down all right,' says the monster. 'Right down into the M drawer!'

'Wait!' says Jill. 'I don't think M is right.'

'I think it's perfect,' says the monster. 'You're a bunch of *meddling* humans. What else could it *possibly* be?'

'Well,' says Jill, 'you *could* file me under G for Girl and Andy and Terry under B for Boys.'

The monster frowns. 'Yes, yes, that's a much better idea.'

It opens the B and G drawers.

'But hang on a minute,' I say. 'You *could* file us under our occupations: me under W for Writer, Terry under I for Illustrator, and Jill under A for Animal rescuer.'

'Or,' says Terry, 'you *could* file us under our names: T for Terry, A for Andy and J for Jill!'

'Or our eye colour,' says Jill. 'B for Blue, G for Green, and H for Hazel.'

'STOP! STOP! STOP!' says the monster. 'You're getting me all confused!'

'Sorry,' says Jill. 'We're just trying to help.'

'Well you're *not* helping,' says the monster. 'But I know what to do. I will cut you all up into pieces and file a piece of you under each of the letters you have suggested. Oh, I am such a clever filing monster! Now where did I put my scissors? Oh yes, here they are … under S, where they belong!'

The monster puts us down and gets out a very large and very sharp-looking pair of scissors.

'Eek!' says Jill.

'Yikes!' says Terry. 'I wish we'd stayed in jail—I'd much rather be in jail than cut into little pieces.'

'Me, too,' I say. 'I never thought I'd say this, but I wish the Story Police were here right now to arrest this crazy monster. Where are they when you *really* need them?'

'We're right here,' says a voice behind us. 'And we're putting a stop to this ridiculous story before it gets any worse and any more crimes are committed. We're putting you ALL under arrest.'

## CHAPTER 12

# THE VERY BIG, VERY DEEP HOLE

We have no choice but to surrender. The Story Police arrest all of us—including the filing monster—and march us down to the beach where their boat is waiting.

'Where are you taking us?' I say.

'To see your old friend, Judge Pumpkin Scones,' says the chief.

'She's not our *friend*,' says Jill. 'She sentenced us to a billion years in prison!'

'It would have been better for you if you'd stayed there,' says the chief. 'This time she's probably going to sentence you to a *zillion* years.'

'But why am *I* under arrest?'
says the monster.

'Because you were about to cut everybody up
with a big pair of scissors!' says the chief. 'Young
children may be reading this book, perhaps even
at bedtime. They don't want to see people being
cut into pieces by monsters—it could give them
terrible nightmares. Now stop arguing,
put those scissors down and get in
the boat with the other prisoners!'

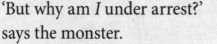

As we climb aboard the boat we see that the
other prisoners are an old man almost bent over
double, a woman with bright-red frizzy hair
wearing a flowerpot on her head, a moose in a
doctor's coat and an angry-looking man with
a really big red nose.

'Excuse me,' says Terry to the man with the big nose, 'you seem familiar. Have we met before?'

'Of course we have, you clown!' says the man. 'It's *me*, your publisher, Mr Big Nose. I should have guessed you two had something to do with this! I'm a busy man, you know—I haven't got time to be arrested for story crimes that I didn't even commit!'

'You published their books,' says the chief. 'You're just as much to blame as anybody—you should have checked them more thoroughly to make sure they didn't break so many story rules.'

'I didn't even know there *were* story rules,' says Mr Big Nose.

'Ignorance of the law is no defence,' says the police chief.

'But what about us?' says the moose, who I am amazed to realise is the one and only Dr Moose, author of *The Splat in the Hat*. 'Why have Beatrix Potty, Boris Bendback and I been arrested?'

'Because,' says the chief, 'your books break lots of rules too, and I believe the children of the world deserve better. I mean, really, what sort of lesson is anyone supposed to learn from ridiculous stories about pooping rabbits, splatting splats and foolish filing monsters?'

'Well,' says Beatrix Potty, 'children can learn a lot of fun facts about nature from my books. For example, some rabbits poop a *lot*!'

'And,' says Boris Bendback, '*Where the Filed Things Are* teaches children that even though there's a place for everything and everything has a place, that place may not necessarily be in a filing cabinet drawer.'

'My book is just supposed to be funny,' says Dr Moose. 'I want to make my readers laugh because, after all, laughter *is* the best medicine … and I should know because as well as being a writer *and* an illustrator, I'm *also* a qualified doctor.'

'Tell it to the judge!' says the chief.

'But I don't have time to tell it to the judge,' says Mr Big Nose. 'I'm a busy man!'

'So am I!' says the chief. 'I have eight prisoners to deliver to the judge and that's exactly what I intend to do.'

'I'm sorry, everybody,' I say. 'It's all my fault. I should never have tried ending Terry's dumb dot story with *and then suddenly we woke up and realised it was all just a dream.* That's what alerted the Story Police in the first place.'

'Don't be so hard on yourself, young fella,' says Boris Bendback. 'What do those Story Police know? Some of the most famous books in the world have ended with waking up and discovering it was all just a dream ... *Alice's Adventures in Wonderland,* for example!'

'And don't forget the *The Wizard of Oz*,' says
Beatrix Potty.

'Thanks,' I say. 'That makes me feel a lot better.
Do you think I should try it again?'

'No,' says Dr Moose quickly. 'Twice in one
book might be a *bit* much.'

'Then what are we going to do?' says Jill.

'Well,' says Mr Big Nose, 'the way I see it, we've got *five* authors and *four* illustrators here. You lot should be able to come up with a creative solution to our problem!'

'Dots!' says Terry. 'They make great holes, remember?'

'Holes?!' I say. 'In a boat? Are you crazy? We'll sink!'

'That's exactly what we *want*,' says Terry. 'If we sink the boat, the Story Police won't be able to take us to jail! Quick: Boris, Dr Moose and Beatrix—help me draw some dots on the bottom of the boat—the more we can draw, the faster we'll sink.'

ship's rat

STORY

'With pleasure!' says Beatrix. 'I love drawing dots!'
'Me too,' says Dr Moose.
'Let the wild dotting begin,' says Boris.

It's not long before water is gushing in through all the newly drawn dot-holes.

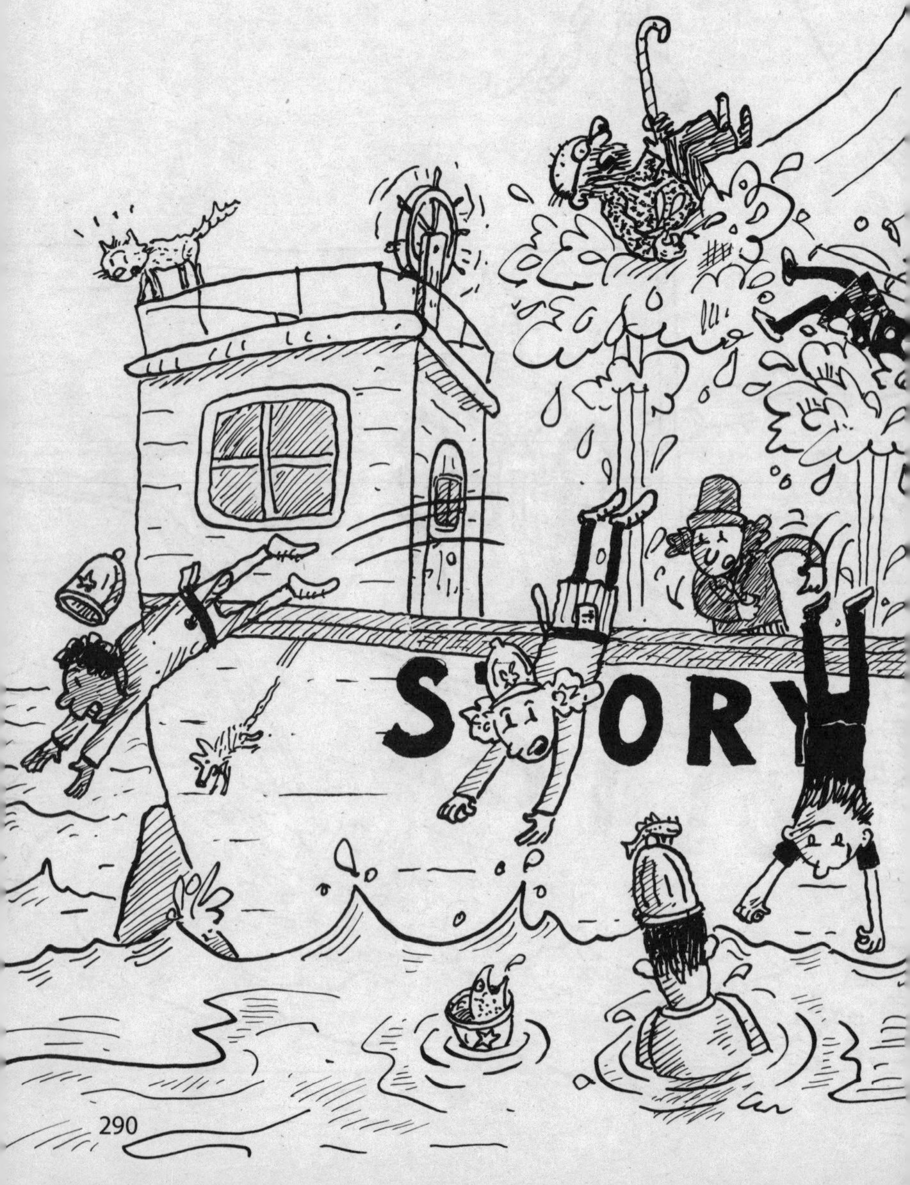
STORY

'Abandon ship!' yells the chief. 'We're taking on water! Abandon ship!'

We all jump overboard and splash our way back towards the shore.

We drag ourselves out of the water and up onto the sand.

'Yay!' says Terry. 'My plan worked. We escaped from the Story Police!'

'Well, yes,' I say, 'but not for long. Look! They're coming!'

Terry turns and sees the Story Police advancing towards us.

'Don't worry about it,' he says. 'I've got an idea for another story—and this one has a really good ending!'

Terry clears his throat and begins narrating:

Once upon a time on an island, Terry, Andy, Jill, Mr Big Nose, Dr Moose, Beatrix Potty, Boris Bendback and a filing monster were surrounded by a load of angry Story Police who wanted to arrest them and put them into storytelling jail for a zillion years. So the brave hero Terry drew a dot ...

and the dot
got bigger ...

and bigger ...

and bigger ...

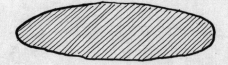

And then it stretched out
and got even bigger ...

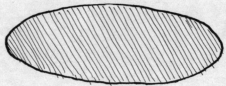

and deeper ...

and bigger and deeper ...

until it became a
really big, really
deep hole ...

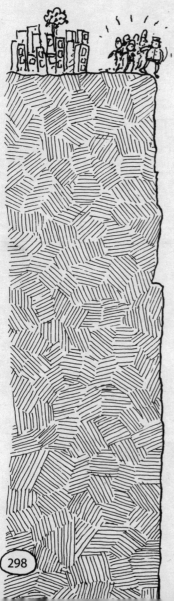

and the Story Police all fell in ...

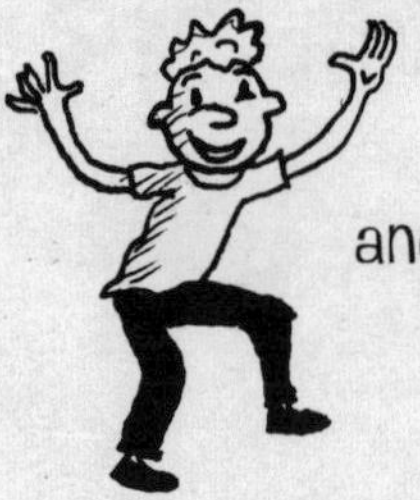

and they all lived happily ever after.

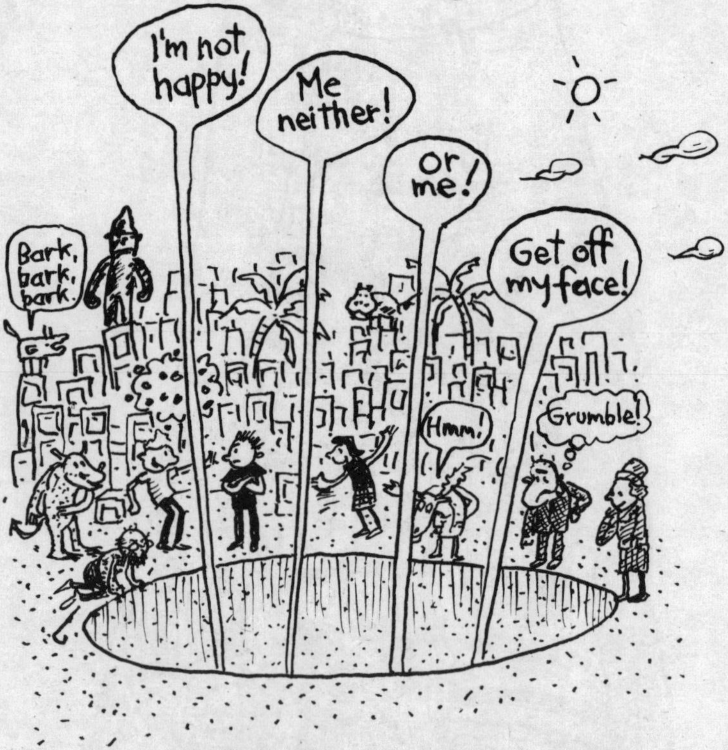
I'm not happy!
Me neither!
Or me!
Get off my face!
Bark, bark, bark.
Hmm!
Grumble!

# THE END!

'HOORAY!' shouts Dr Moose. 'Now all the storytellers of the world are free to tell whatever stories they want without fear of the Story Police!'

Terry peels the hole off the ground and gives it to the filing monster.

'You might like to file this under H for Hole,' he says.

'I'd love to!' says the monster. 'And after I've done that I'll get on with filing the rest of the island just the way it was.'

'Please don't file any animals,' says Jill. 'They don't like it.'

'Or trees,' I say.

'Or rocks or sand,' says Terry.

'What?!' says the monster. 'You mean I should just let it all lie around in a big mess?'

'Yes,' says Jill. 'It's called *nature* and it's the way it's meant to be!'

'But I'm a *filing* monster,' says the monster, looking sad. 'What will I do if I can't file?'

'Well,' says Mr Big Nose, 'I could use an enthusiastic filing monster like you in my office at Big Nose Books.'

'Oh, that would be wonderful,' says the monster. 'I always wanted to get into publishing. It starts with P, one of my favourite letters.'

Terry giggles. 'P,' he says.

'So,' says Mr Big Nose, 'what happens now? I need
to get back to work. I'm a busy man, you know.
And you need to get your book done by five o'clock
today … or else!'

'We can all sail home on your dot-yacht, can't we,
Terry?' says Jill.

'No,' I say. 'It's not there any more. One-eyed Pete stole it.'

'I hate pirates,' sighs Terry.

'So what are we going to do?' says Jill. 'How will we get home?'

Terry strokes his chin thoughtfully. 'If only we had a cane basket,' he says, 'and a little bit of fire. I could inflate a dot and turn it into a hot-air balloon.'

'I have some fire filed under F,' says the filing monster. 'And a cane basket under B ... here you are!'

'Thanks!' says Terry.

Terry draws a dot and attaches it to the basket.

'Everyone climb in,' he says.

We all pile into the basket and Terry uses the heat from the fire to inflate the dot.

As the dot rises into the air, the ropes tighten and lift the basket off the ground.

'We'll be home in no time,' says Terry. 'Then we can get started on our book.'

'The sooner we get started, the better,' I say. 'There's a lot for us to write about. So much has happened today!'

'Dr Moose and Boris and I could help,' says Beatrix. 'After all, we can all write *and* illustrate.'

'Of course,' says Dr Moose. 'You know what they say: Many hooves make light work.'

'I couldn't agree more,' says Boris. 'And I'd love to visit your treehouse—I've read so much about it!'

'And I'd like to come and meet all your animals, Jill,' says Beatrix.

'And they would love to meet you,' says Jill. 'They're big fans of your books!'

'Well, that's settled then,' I say, as the hot-air dot rises higher and higher into the air. 'You're all invited to visit and help us with our book!'

'Up, up and away!' says Terry.

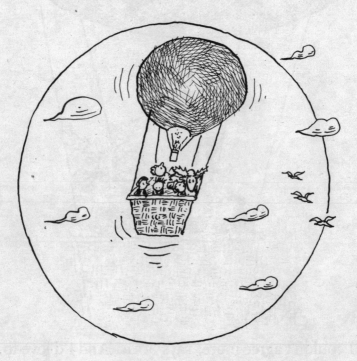

## CHAPTER 13

# THE LAST CHAPTER

We float up … and up …

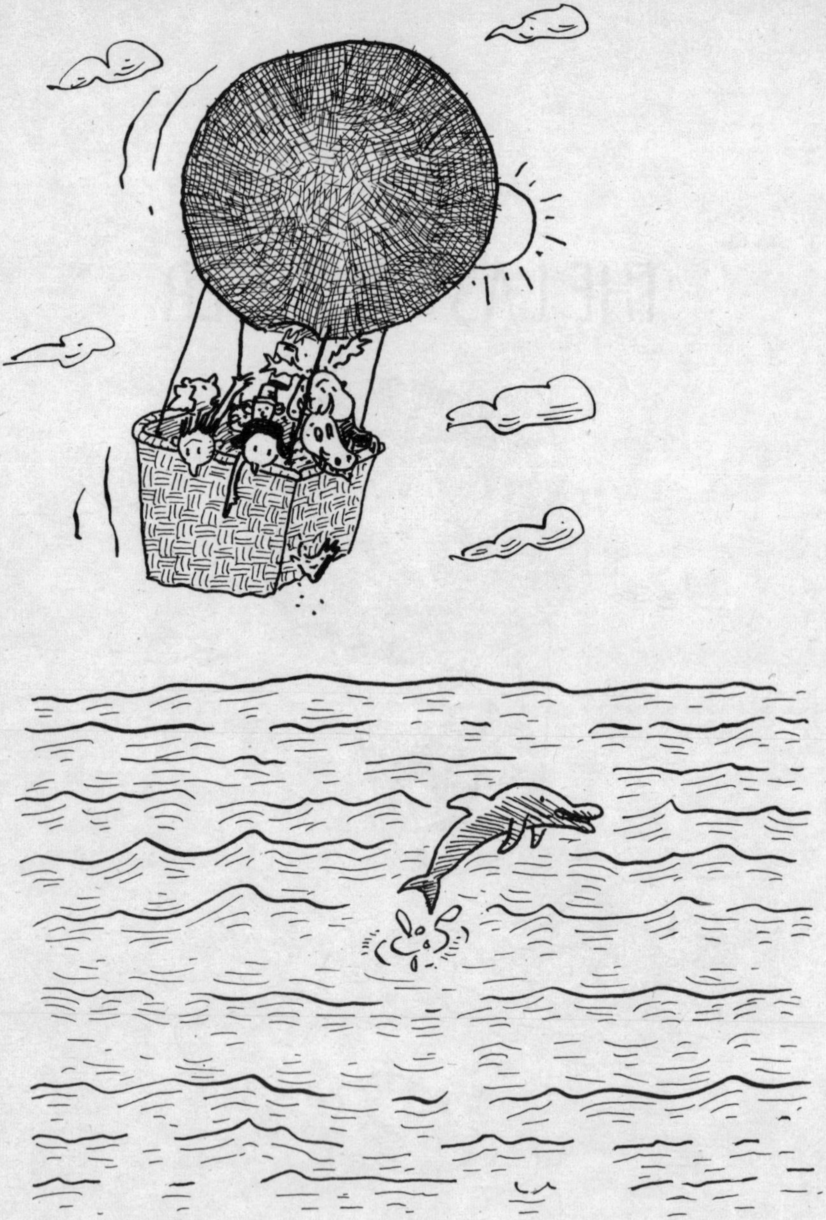

and away …

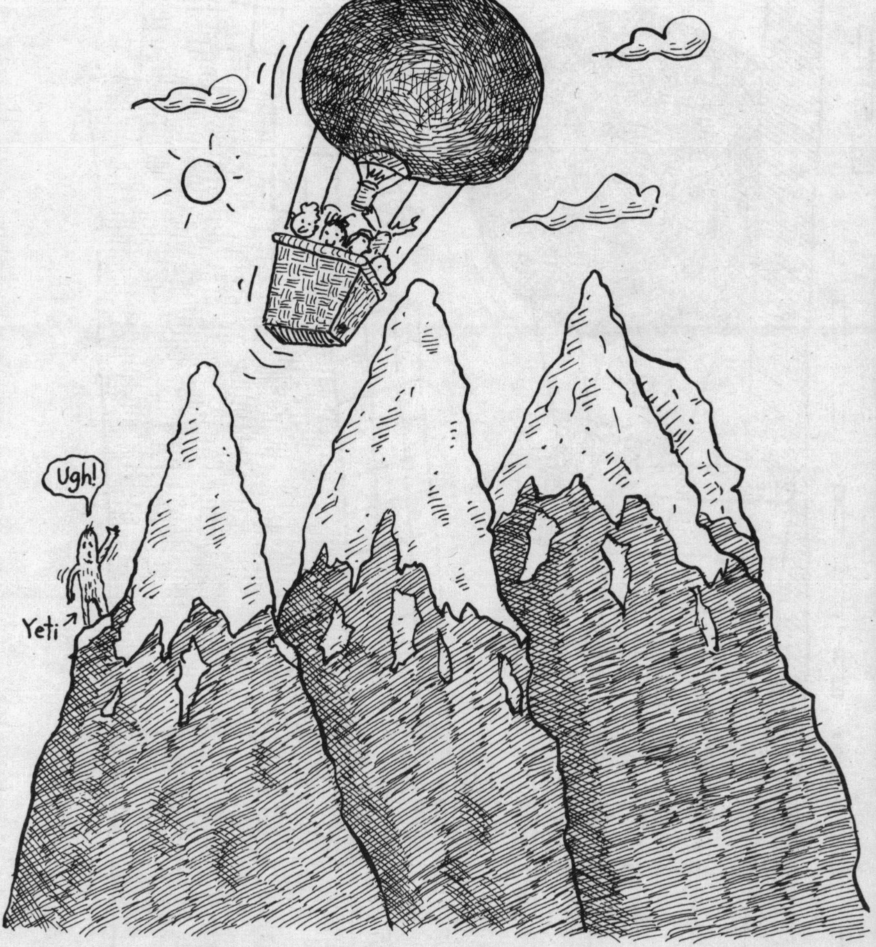
Ugh!
Yeti

and away …

until, eventually, we come to the city.

We drop Mr Big Nose and the filing monster off at Big Nose Books.

'Thanks for the ride,' says the filing monster as we float away.

'And don't forget,' yells Mr Big Nose, 'your manuscript is due at five o'clock … OR ELSE!'

We float on a little further and finally, at long last, we are home.

'What an absolutely splendidly stupendous treehouse you have here!' says Dr Moose.

'Yes, I've never seen one quite like it,' says Boris Bendback.

'Do we have time to look around before we start work?' says Beatrix Potty.

'Of course,' I say. 'We can take you on a tour of the main attractions in our penguin-powered flying treehouse tour bus!'

Jill gives Boris, Beatrix and Dr Moose a ticket each.

'Tickets, please!' says Jill, collecting the tickets as they climb aboard the bus.

Terry gets in the driver's seat and I put on my treehouse tour guide hat and start the tour.

'Welcome aboard!' I say, as we take off. 'Our treehouse has one hundred and seventeen levels. Some are fun, some are scary, some are fun *and* scary, and some are scary *and* fun.'

'Do you have any food?' says Boris Bendback. 'I'm famished!'

Me, too!

'Of course we do!' I say. 'We have ice-cream, lollipops, popcorn, marshmallows, pizza, submarine sandwiches and a chocolate waterfall—you can swim *and* eat at the same time.'

'Do you have anything a little more filling?' says
Boris Bendback. 'I'm *so* hungry I could eat a couch.'

'We have just the thing,' I say. 'Terry, take us to the
all-you-can-eat-including-the-furniture level.'

'Roger that,' says Terry.

On the all-you-can-eat-including-the-furniture level Dr Moose pulls some daffodils from a vase and eats them. Then he crunches up the vase as well.

Beatrix chews on a chocolate-coated chair.

Boris eats a whole couch. 'Ah,' he says, licking his lips, 'just like the couches Mother used to bake!'

Terry, Jill and I end up eating everything else.

'Being chased by the Story Police sure does give you an appetite,' I say.

'Roger that,' says Terry.

'Well,' I say, 'let's get on with the tour.'

We all file back onto the bus and continue the
tour. We tour high.

We tour low.

We tour fast.

We tour slow.

We go …

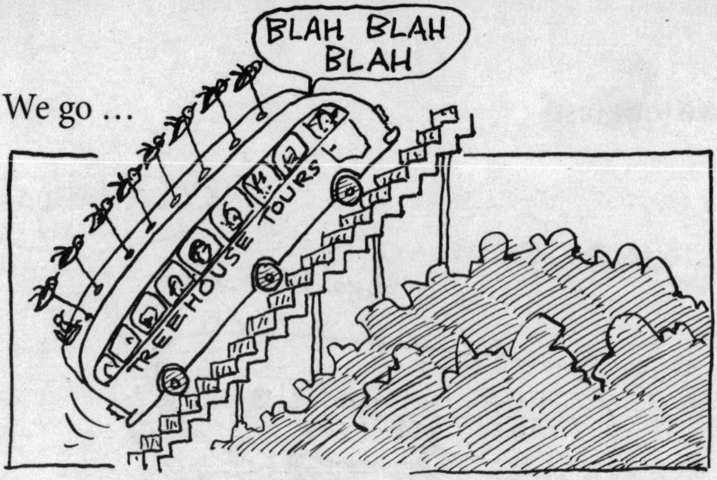
BLAH BLAH BLAH
TREEHOUSE TOURS

and we go …

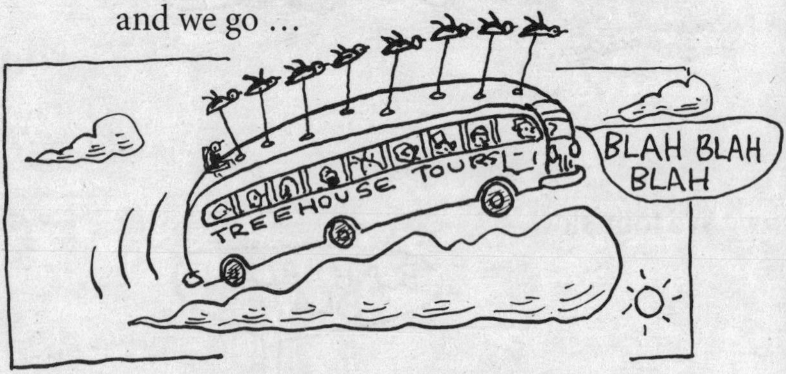
BLAH BLAH BLAH
TREEHOUSE TOURS

and we go …

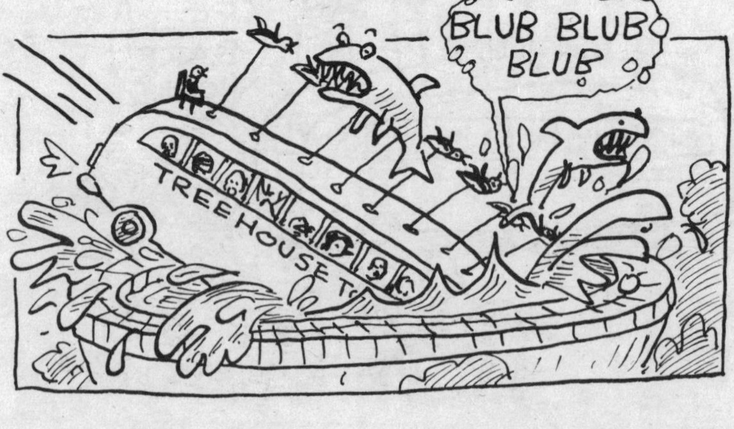
BLUB BLUB BLUB
TREEHOUSE

and we go.

'STOP!' says Dr Moose, pointing at our beautiful sunny meadow full of buttercups, butterflies and bluebirds. 'Can we land down there?'

'Of course!' I say.

Terry parks the bus and we all get out.

'Oh, look!' says Beatrix. 'A family of field mice!
Stay still, my little friends, while I sketch you.'

Boris Bendback lies on his stomach in a patch of buttercups. 'My, this sun is doing my back a power of good,' he says.

'Yippee, I'm free!' says Dr Moose, galloping off across the meadow as fast as his thundering hooves can carry him.

'Dr Moose!' I yell. 'STOP!'

But Dr Moose just keeps going … and going … and going.

'I hope he comes back in time to help us write the book,' says Terry.

'Not when he gets like this, he won't,' says Beatrix, looking up from her sketching. 'He can run for days, you know. He may be a doctor and an accomplished author-illustrator, but he's also a wild animal.'

'I think I can get him back with my moose-lasso,' says Jill, pulling a long piece of rope out of her portable animal-rescue kit.

Jill swings the rope expertly around her head and then lets it fly.

It sails across the meadow, and snares Dr Moose around the antlers.

Jill drags Dr Moose back to the bus.

'Sorry about that,' says Dr Moose, panting. 'Once I get going I just can't stop myself.'

'No need to apologise,' I say, as the bus takes off. 'Now, if you look down there, you'll see our giant-fighting-robot arena.'

'Giant fighting *robots*?' says Beatrix. 'Can we have a go?'

'Are you sure?' I say. 'The giant-fighting-robot suits are pretty dangerous.'

'Danger is my middle name,' says Beatrix.

'Mine too,' says Dr Moose.

'Mine as well!' says Boris.

And without waiting for permission, or for Terry to land, all three leap from the windows of the bus.

By the time we land, Beatrix, Boris and Dr Moose are suited up and ready to rumble.

They circle each other warily until I ding the bell ... and then the fight is on!

DING!

← Post

Discarded uniform + hat

Page number

KICK!

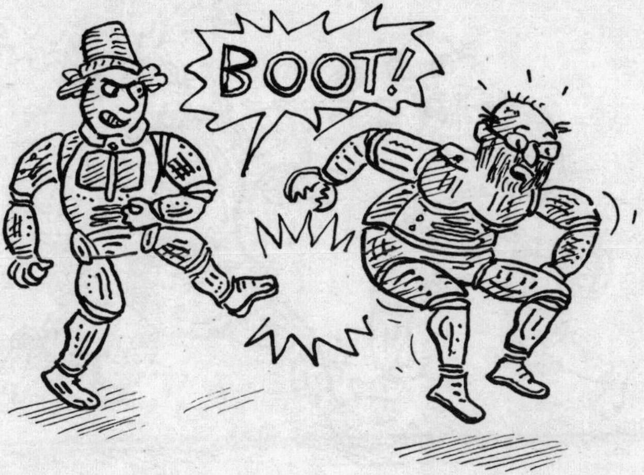
BOOT!

PUNCH!

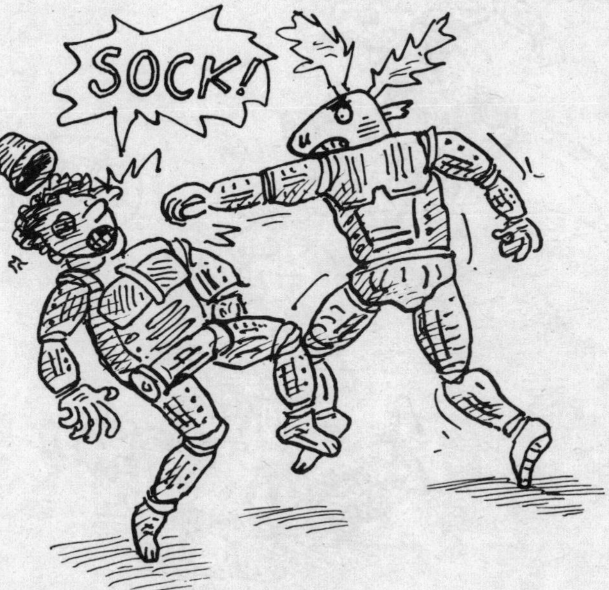
SOCK!

STOMP!

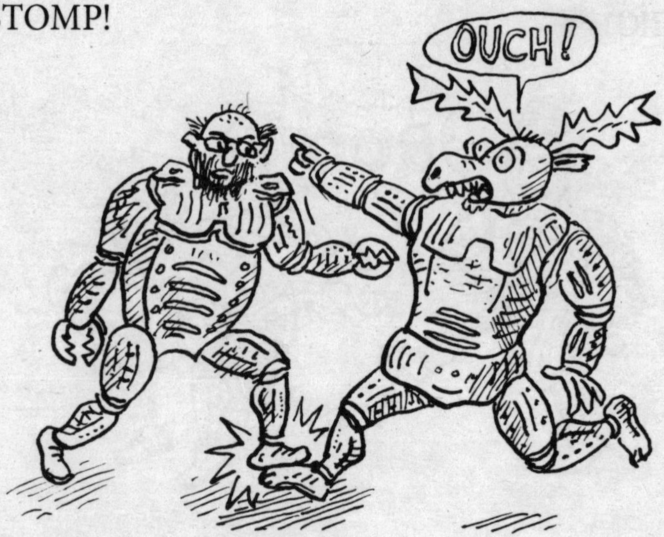
OUCH!

CRUSH!

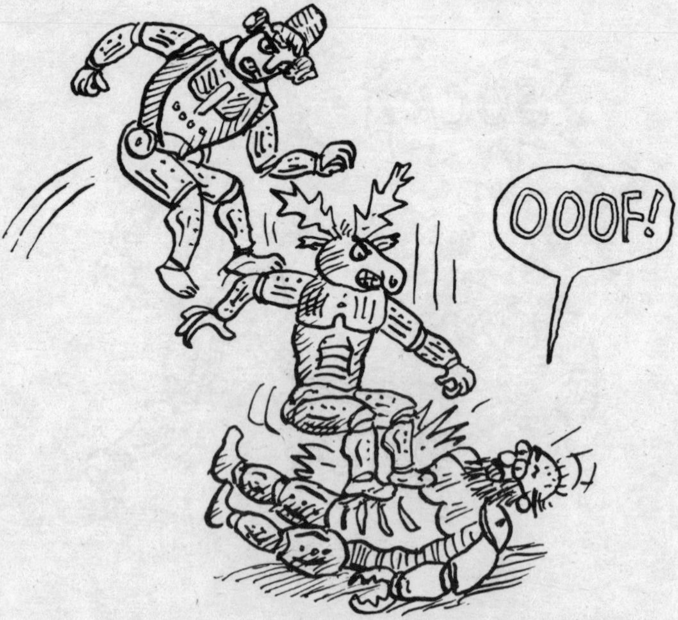
OOOF!

THROW!

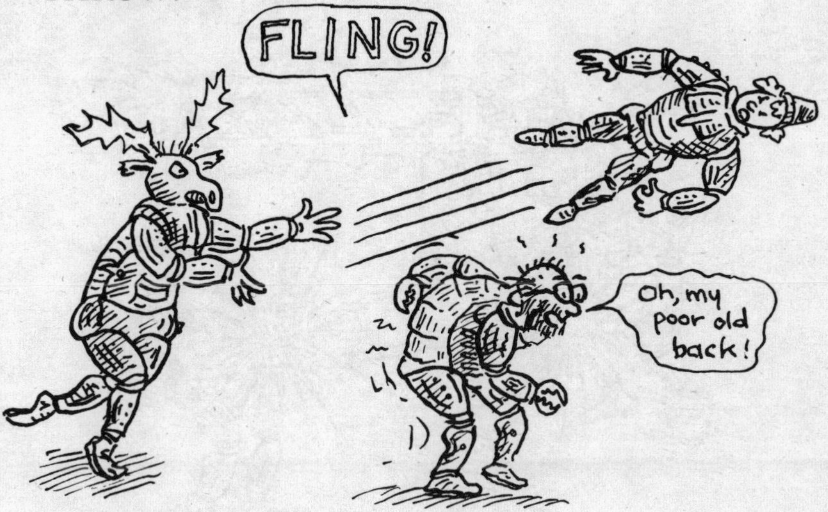
FLING!
Oh, my poor old back!

POUND!

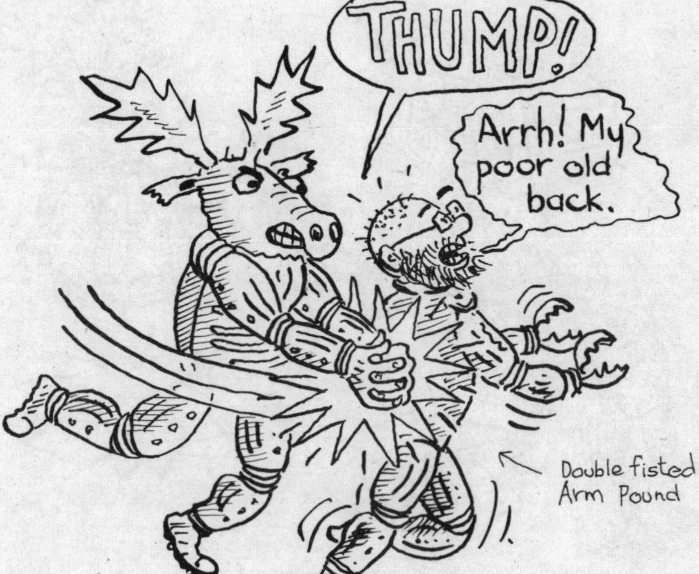
THUMP!
Arrh! My poor old back.
Double fisted Arm Pound

They blast each other with laser beams …

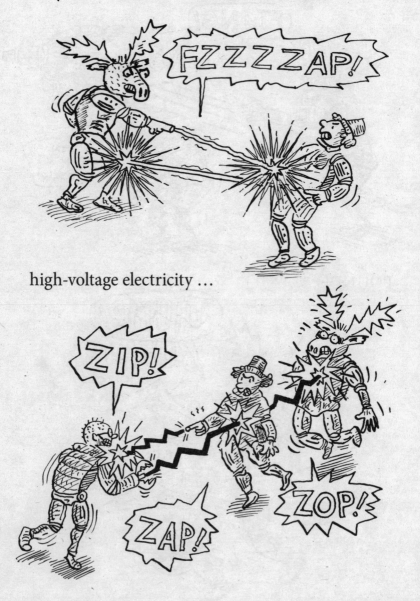

high-voltage electricity …

and fireballs!

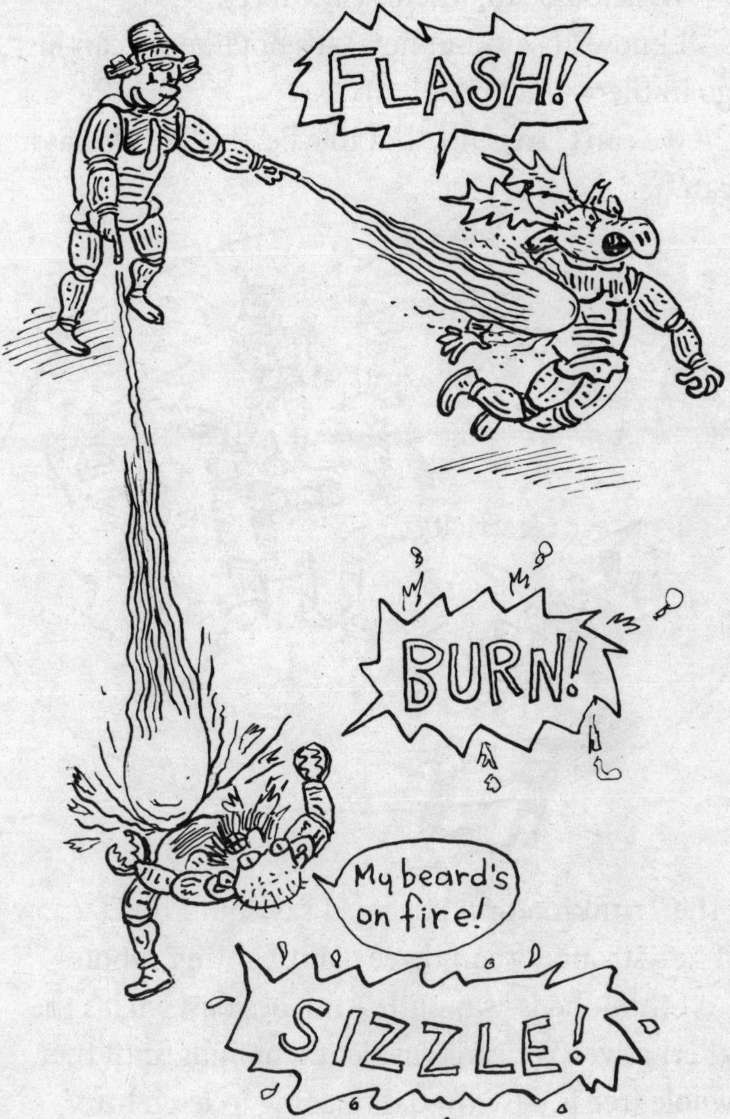
FLASH!
BURN!
My beard's on fire!
SIZZLE!

The whole tree is shuddering and shaking.

'We should stop them,' says Terry.

'I know!' I say. 'But how? It's not like we can just go in there and break it up.'

'*We* can't,' says Jill, 'but maybe The Trunkinator can.'

'The Trunkinator *is* strong,' I say, 'but I don't know if he's stronger than three giant fighting robots.'

'I think he is,' says Jill. 'And, besides, what's the alternative? We can't just let them fight until the whole tree is destroyed. I'm going to fetch him.'

Jill comes back with The Trunkinator and whispers instructions in his ear.

The Trunkinator leaps into the ring. Robo-Beatrix, Robo-Boris and Robo-Dr Moose stop fighting with each other and turn to face their new opponent.

Robo-Boris steps forward. 'Put up your duke!' he says.

'I can't watch!' says Jill, covering her eyes.

Boris Bendback is definitely asking for it, and The Trunkinator certainly lets him have it.

PUNCH!

With one punch of his mighty trunk he sends Boris flying out of his robot suit, up into the air ...

and down onto the watermelon-smashing level.

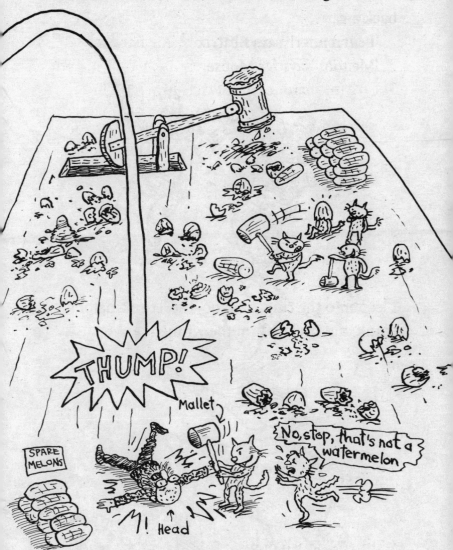

Robo-Beatrix and Robo-Dr Moose immediately back away.

'I surrender!' says Beatrix.

'Me too!' says Dr Moose.

I leap into the ring, hold up The Trunkinator's trunk and declare him the winner.

Beatrix and Dr Moose get out of their robot suits
and rush to the watermelon-smashing level.

We fly over and land the bus next to Boris, who
is lying motionless beside a pile of un-smashed
watermelons.

Beatrix is kneeling beside him, fanning his face.

'Are you okay, Boris?' says Beatrix.

'Never felt better!' says Boris, suddenly leaping up and stretching out to his full height.

'The Trunkinator punched me so hard he *un*-bent my back! I haven't felt so good in years!'

'Me neither!' says Dr Moose.

We look around to see him enthusiastically smashing watermelons.

'I've always wanted to smash a watermelon,' he says, 'and now I have!'

'Can we smash some watermelons, too?' says Beatrix.

'Well,' I say, 'it's not an official part of the tour, but since we're here we may as well—after all, those watermelons aren't going to smash themselves!'

He, he!

'Well, this is a lot of fun,' I say, 'but we've got a book to make! Mallets down, everybody. It's time to get back on the bus.'

Our visitors resume their seats and Jill hands out hot towels so everybody can clean themselves up.

We fly through the branches at top speed and land in our high-tech office. We all leave the bus, grab pencils, pens, paint, paintbrushes and paper, and set to work …

# authoring and illustrating …

# and illustrating and authoring …

and illustrator-authoring …

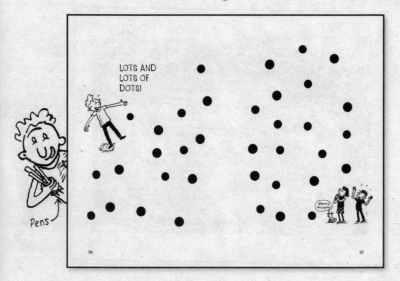

and author-illustrating …

# and author-illustrator-authoring …

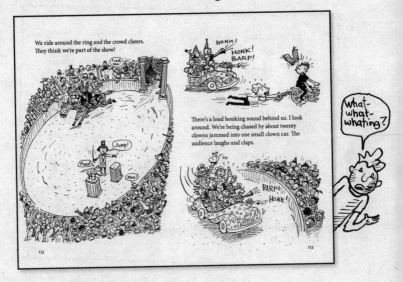

# and illustrator-author-illustrating …

## and illustrator-author authoring …

## and author-illustrator illustrating …

and author-illustrator illustrating *and* authoring …

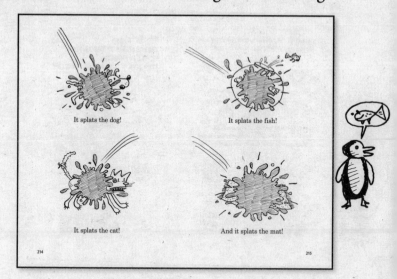

and illustrator-author authoring *and* illustrating …

## and author-illustrator author-illustrating …

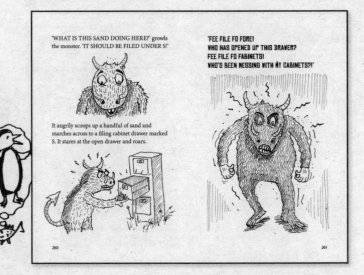

'WHAT IS THIS SAND DOING HERE?' growls the monster. 'IT SHOULD BE FILED UNDER S!'

It angrily scoops up a handful of sand and marches across to a filing cabinet drawer marked S. It stares at the open drawer and roars.

'FEE FILE FO FORE!
WHO HAS OPENED UP THIS DRAWER?
FEE FILE FO FABINETS!
WHO'S BEEN MESSING WITH MY CABINETS?!'

260

261

## and illustrator-author illustrator-authoring …

It's not long before water starts gushing in through all the newly drawn dot-holes. The boat is sinking rapidly.

'Abandon ship!' yells the chief. 'We're taking on water! Abandon ship!'
We all jump overboard and splash our way back towards the shore.

290

291

358

and author-illustrator illustrating author-illustrator illustrating-authoring … until it's all finished!

'That was fun!' says Boris. 'But how are we going to get it to your publisher in time? It's almost five o'clock!'

'Couldn't you use your tour bus to deliver it?' says Dr Moose.

'I'm afraid not,' says Jill. 'The penguins are tired and need a rest.'

'Never fear,' says Terry. 'I could make a *drot*.'

'What's a drot?' I say.

'It's a remote-controlled dot,' says Terry. 'Like a drone, but more dotty. Here, I'll show you.'

'Oh, how cute!' says Dr Moose.

'Yes!' says Jill. 'It looks like a little animal! Does it have a name?'

'It's called *Drot*,' says Terry. 'And it may be cute, but it has a very important job to do.'

Terry attaches the manuscript to Drot and picks up the remote control. Drot rises into the air and zips out of the treehouse.

'We can track its progress on Drot-cam,' Terry says.

We gather around the Drot-cam screen and watch as Drot travels over the forest …

across the
city ...

in through
Mr Big Nose's
office window ...

and
lands on
his desk.

'Excellent,' says Mr Big Nose. 'Five o'clock, right on the *drot*!'

'I'll deal with it immediately, sir,' says the filing monster. 'I'll file the drot under D and the manuscript under M.'

'Well, that worked out quite nicely,' says Terry.

'Yes,' I say. 'I hate to admit it, but your dumb dot story wasn't so dumb after all.'

'I agree,' says Jill. 'In fact, I think it's the *un*-dumbest dumb dot story I've ever heard.'

'Thanks,' says Terry. 'Hey, Andy, do you think we could make a dot level in the treehouse?'

'You mean a level where there's nothing *but* dots?' I say.

'Yeah,' says Terry. 'A non-stop dot level!'

'Why not?' I say. 'The dots really came through for us in this book. It's the least we could do. We can add it to the list of new storeys for the 130-storey treehouse.'

'Yay,' says Terry. 'Let's get started right away!'

'Hold on,' I say, 'not so fast. Right now we have something much more important to do.'

'What could be *more* important than building the next thirteen storeys of our treehouse?' says Terry.

'Having a pyjama party, that's what,' I say. 'There's one starting in five minutes *and* everyone's invited!'

'Hooray,' says Boris. 'I *love* pyjama parties!'

'So do I!' says Dr Moose.

'Me too!' says Beatrix. 'Can all your animals come as well, Jill?'

'Of course,' says Jill. 'They love pyjama parties!'

'Well, what are we waiting for?' says Terry. 'Let's do it!'

So we do.

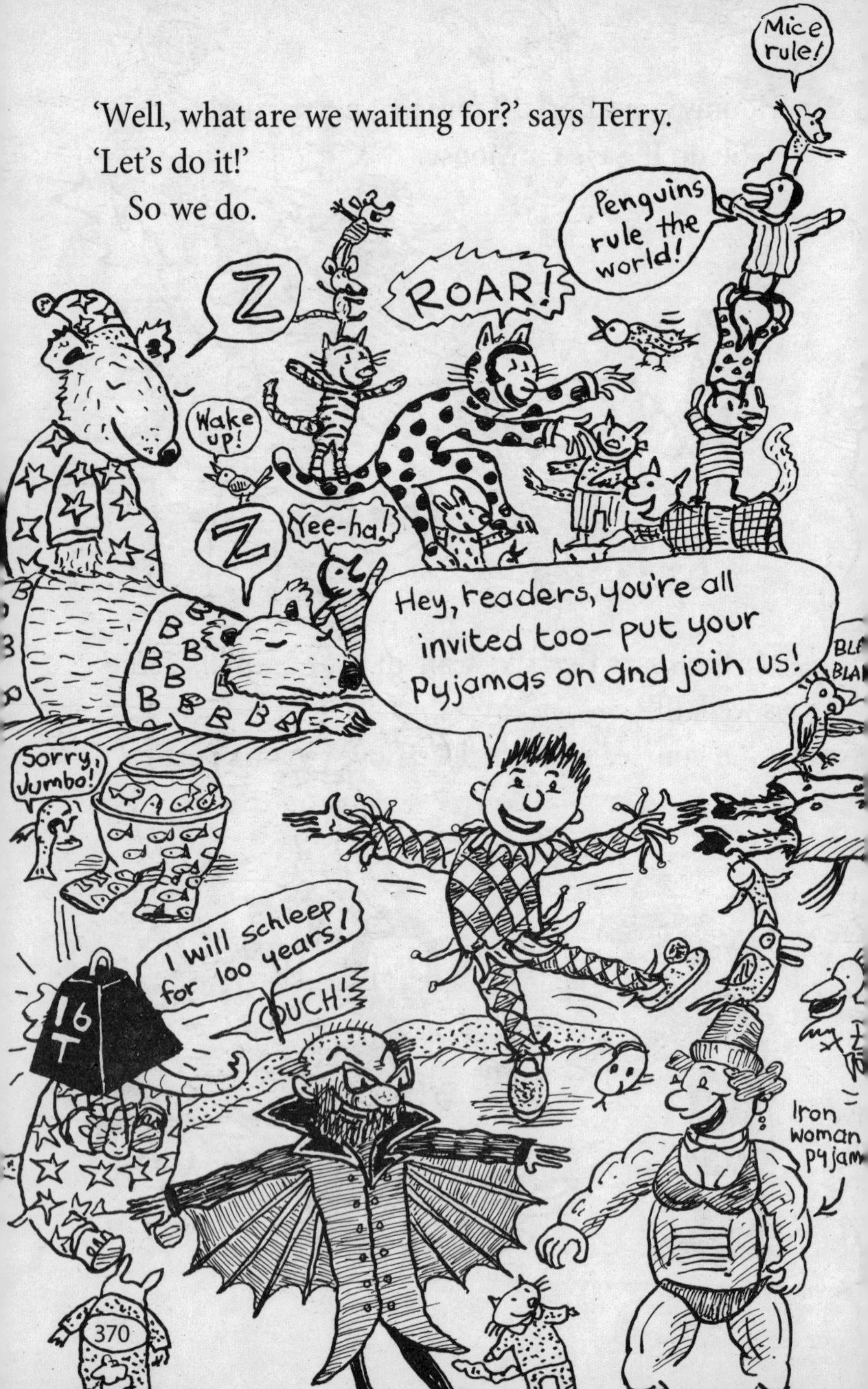
Mice rule!
Penguins rule the world!
Z
ROAR!
Wake up!
Z
Yee-ha!
Hey, readers, you're all invited too – put your pyjamas on and join us!
Sorry, Jumbo!
I will schleep for 100 years!
OUCH!
16 T
Iron woman

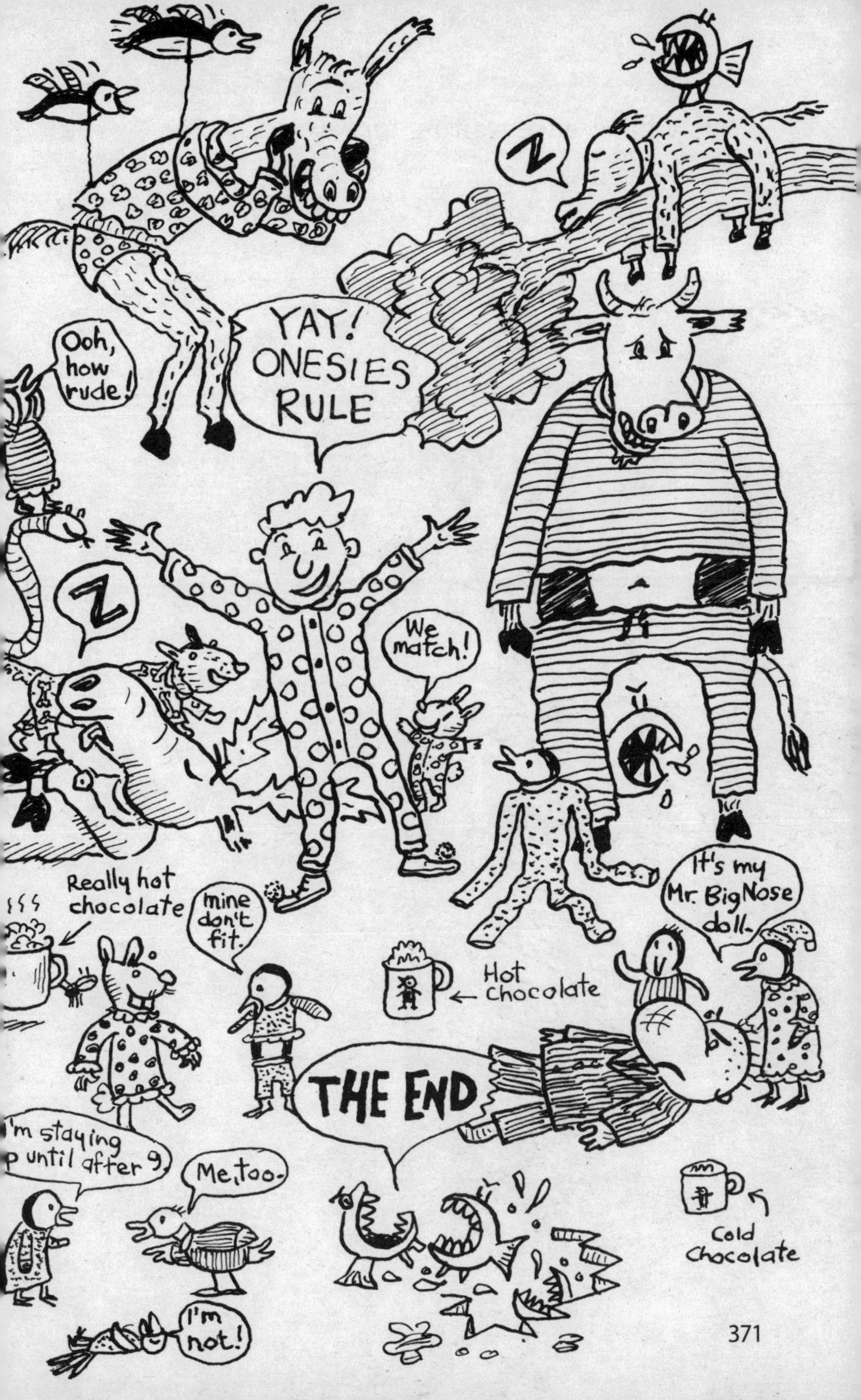

Ooh, how rude!
YAY! ONESIES RULE
We match!
Really hot chocolate
mine don't fit.
Hot chocolate
It's my Mr. BigNose doll.
THE END
I'm staying up until after 9.
Me, too.
I'm not!
Cold Chocolate

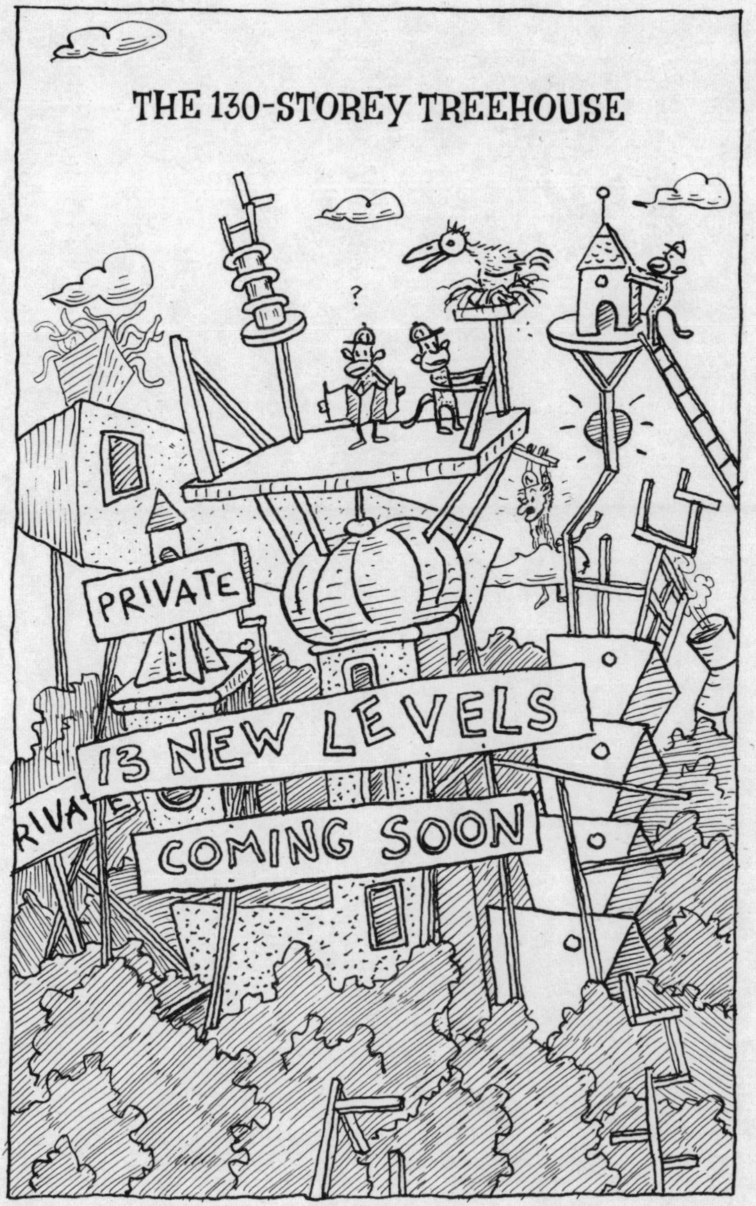
THE 130-STOREY TREEHOUSE
?
PRIVATE
13 NEW LEVELS
COMING SOON

# CLIMB HIGHER EVERY TIME
# WITH THE TREEHOUSE SERIES

# LOTS OF LAUGHS AT EVERY LEVEL!

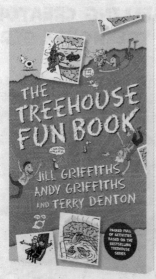

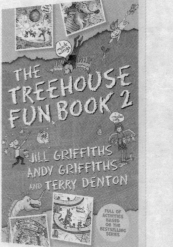

**COMING SOON**
**FROM THE INTERNATIONALLY**
**BESTSELLING CREATORS OF**
**THE TREEHOUSE SERIES**

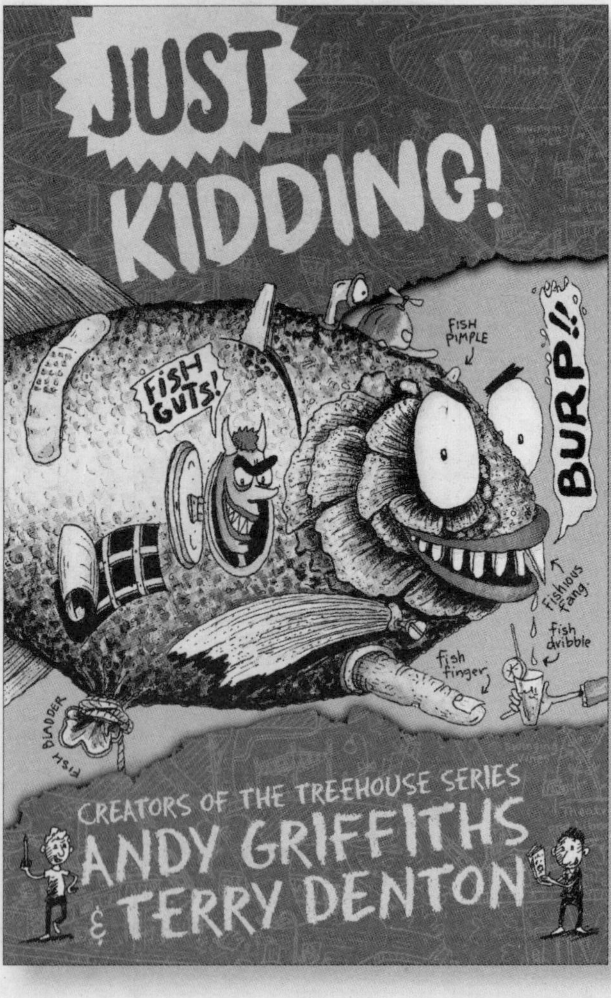
JUST
KIDDING!
FISH GUTS!
FISH PIMPLE
BURP!!
Fishious Fang.
fish dribble
fish finger
FISH BLADDER
CREATORS OF THE TREEHOUSE SERIES
ANDY GRIFFITHS
& TERRY DENTON